Mark Twain in Love

Mark Twain in Love

ALBERT G. MILLER

New York

Harcourt Brace Jovanovich, Inc.

The author wishes to thank Harper & Row, Publishers, Inc., for permission to use short Mark Twain quotations from the following books published by them: *Mark Twain, a Biography* by Albert Bigelow Paine; *The Love Letters of Mark Twain,* edited by Dixon Wecter; *Mark Twain's Autobiography,* with an introduction by Albert Bigelow Paine; *Mark Twain's Letters,* arranged by Albert Bigelow Paine; and "The Private History of a Campaign that Failed" from *The Family Mark Twain.*

Printed in the United States of America
First edition
B C D E F G H I J K

Library of Congress Cataloging in Publication Data

Miller, Albert G 1905–
    Mark Twain in love.

    SUMMARY: A fictionalized reconstruction of Mark
Twain's courtship of Livy Langdon.
    1. Clemens, Samuel Langhorne, 1835–1910—Juvenile
fiction. [1. Clemens, Samuel Langhorne, 1835–1910—
Fiction] I. Title.
PZ7.M6113Mar   [Fic]   73–5243
ISBN 0–15–230295–6

For Mary Sue

AUTHOR'S NOTE

When writing Mark Twain's love story in fictional form, it was necessary to invent conversations not recorded in published accounts of his life.

Also, in keeping with the fictional character of the narrative, several imagined scenes and embellishments were added.

The chronology of Mark's Elmira campaign, however, was not altered, and the principal events of his courtship actually occurred as noted in the story.

Mark Twain in Love

1

IT was clear to Samuel Clemens, as he trudged along the brick sidewalk from the horsecar stop, that St. Louis, Missouri, had not changed noticeably during the six years since he had last been back to visit his mother. On this soft April night in 1867, it seemed still pretty much as he had known it: a smoky industrial city on the edge of the mile-wide highway of the Mississippi.

His mother's house on the heights above the levee had not changed, either, as he was presently to discover.

Sam himself, however, had acquired vast new dimensions and equipment during his thirteen years of roving. A printer in eastern cities in his early manhood, he had subsequently become a skilled river pilot on the steamboat run from St. Louis to New Orleans. Following the outbreak of the war, in 1861, he had added not only three occupations—mining, journalism, and lecturing—but also a striking new name—Mark Twain. The pseudonym was already famous in the West and fast gaining respectful recognition clear across the country. Sam used it when lecturing and had signed it to an immensely popular story about a contest between jumping frogs.

Returning now as a successful, experienced man of thirty-one, Sam Clemens—Mark Twain—was a genuine, dyed-in-the-wool example of one of America's most admired characters—the boy who made good.

In the parlor of her two-story frame house, the sharp ping of the clock on the mantel startled Jane Clemens from a doze. "My land," she muttered, jerking her head up, "what's gone with me, I wonder." In the circle of yellow light thrown by the kerosene lamp, she saw that it was half-past nine. Biting off a thread, she rose briskly and draped a nearly finished patchwork quilt over the back of the rocker.

Sam Clemens's mother, at sixty-four, was spry and mentally alert, and followed certain habit patterns that seldom varied. Initiating her bedtime routine, she placed the lamp on the mantel, where it illuminated a row of patent medicines. Squinting at the labels through her half-moon spectacles, she uncorked one of the bottles, poured out a spoonful of green liquid, and swallowed it without hesitation. From another bottle she filled the spoon with a viscous red dose and downed it with similar dispatch and satisfaction.

A draft from a third bottle was poured out, but as Jane raised it to her mouth, her eye was caught by a brown leaf hanging limply from one of the rubber plants in the front window. Clucking her annoyance, she carried the spoon carefully across the room and dripped the elixir onto the base of the plant's stem.

"There, mister," she said, yanking off the dead leaf, "that'll teach you not to look sickly in my house."

Following a dose for herself from the third bottle, Jane hefted a huge tomcat from a corner of the sofa, opened the front door, and put him out, sending him on his way with an affectionate paddle on the rear.

"Good night, Absalom," she called after him. "Have a good time."

"Thanks, Mrs. Clemens," came a high-pitched voice from the darkness. "I'll sure try."

Startled, Jane stepped back into the room, then quickly recovered herself and called out, "Sam-*ee!*" Receiving no answer, she gave a stern command: "Samuel Langhorne Clemens—you come in here this minute!"

"Mee—yow-w-w!" Sam yowled as he appeared, grinning, in the doorway.

Sparsely built, never brawny or robust like so many of the miners he knew in the West, Sam Clemens was about five feet ten, with a large head crowned by dark reddish-brown hair and decorated with a huge brush of a moustache. His blue eyes, half hidden by luxuriant brows, were keen and twinkling.

Stepping into the room, Sam closed the door with his heel and dropped his burdens—a battered valise, a yellow duster, and a rolled umbrella.

"Sammy, you bad boy," his mother scolded, "you almost gave me a fit with your caterwauling."

Enjoying his joke, he embraced her and spoke with

his familiar, lazy drawl. "I really sold you, didn't I, Ma?"

"You good-for-nothing scamp," she said in mock anger. "Rightly I ought to box your ears." Stepping back a little, she frowned up at him.

"What's wrong?" Sam asked.

"Your face."

"What about my face?"

"It's changed since I saw it last."

"No wonder," he said wryly. "It's got six more years of wear and tear in it. In that length of time, I guess everything changes." He looked at the clock. "Sorry to get here so late, Ma, but it couldn't be helped."

"I'm happy you got here at all. I'd about given you up for the day."

"Blame it on that miserable railroad. Forty-six hours from New York. I could've made it a lot sooner in a baby buggy."

His mother scanned his face for signs of starvation. "You must be wolf-hungry, Sammy. Can I fry you an egg, or maybe a pork chop?"

He winced. "No thanks. After that rocky ride, my insides just want to be ignored for a spell."

"Ah!" She raised a forefinger and rushed to the mantel. "What you need, sonny, is a good stummick-settler. I got a brand-new one here that works magic."

Sam chuckled. "I see *you* haven't changed."

She handed him one of the bottles. "Here. A dose of this will fix you up in a jiffy."

He examined the label. " 'Dr. Osgool's India Chol-agogue.' I swear, Ma, there never was a quack medicine in Brown's drugstore back home in Hannibal that you didn't sample. It's a wonder your plumbing hasn't surrendered long ago."

Jane bristled. "I'm a sight healthier than *you* are, Sam Clemens."

"I don't doubt it. My innards have been going downhill ever since I was an infant. All because you weaned me on these balms, bitters, and balsams." With a slight shudder, he set the bottle down.

"You can thank your stars I did look after you. You were a mighty sickly young 'un, and puny, too. Kept me busy day and night, nursin' you and fussin' over you."

"I reckon you enjoyed it, Ma."

"Not much I didn't. You caused me more uneasiness than any child I ever had." She settled herself in the rocker. "Never gave me a peaceful minute. Whenever you were in the house, you near drove me crazy with your didoes. And when you were out of it, gallivantin' around, I was always expectin' that somebody'd bring you home half dead."

"Well, I didn't disappoint you on that score. I mind the time I was fished out of the river and deposited right inside the front door in a limp, soggy condition. Remember?"

"Land yes—like it was yesterday. Seems like you had half the Mississippi inside you. After I emptied you out

15

I put you to bed and dosed you with mullen tea and castor oil."

"Yes, and the treatment was a danged sight worse than the ailment."

Jane pointed to a chair. "Do you have to stand up like that? Sit down and be comfortable."

"No thanks, Ma. I've been avoiding chairs ever since last year, when I came back from the Sandwich Islands with a flourishing crop of saddle boils." He gave his posterior a gentle rub. "My keel still hasn't recovered, so I stand up as much as possible. Of course that fits right in with my new profession of lecturing. On the lecture platform I'm obliged to stand."

"You wrote me about all that public speakin' you've been doin' out west. It must be right tirin', keepin' it up night after night."

"It is, Ma, but I enjoy every minute of it."

She nodded. "I don't doubt it. You always did like to show off in front of people."

Upon his return from the Sandwich Islands, about which he had written a series of letters for a Sacramento newspaper, Sam had been at loose ends and in need of money. Already an entertaining talker, he was advised by a friend to deliver a lecture about the islands for pay. Billed as Mark Twain, he did so with resounding success and followed it with more lectures, delighting audiences in such places as San Francisco, Sacramento, You Bet, Red Dog, Gold Hill, and Grass Valley.

Heretofore in his letters to his mother, his sister Pa-

16

mela, and his brother Orion, he had been "Sam." But lately, more often than not, he had signed himself "Mark," which testified to his growing fame.

"You plan to keep right on lecturin'?" Jane asked.

"Sure, unless they start throwing eggs at me. My first talk in the East is set for next month in New York City, and to tell you the truth, Ma, it scares me a little."

"Don't worry about it, son. You'll do fine," she assured him. "You'll always do fine at everything you try —I feel it in my bones."

"Thanks, I hope your bones don't lie."

Jane sighed. "I only wish I could have that same feelin' about your brother. Poor Orion, he's always chasin' phantoms—always schemin' to get rich quick. That's why he'll never have a penny to his name."

Sam sat down gingerly and took out a cigar. "I was going to ask you about Orion. Does he write you?"

"I had a letter from him just last week."

While Sam bit off the end of the cigar and lighted it, his mother packed a corncob pipe, struck a match, and puffed the tobacco to a glow. Resting contentedly in a cloud of smoke, they resumed the conversation.

"What's Orion up to this time?" Sam asked.

"Nothin' that's practical. But he did say he's changed his religion again. Now he's gone Methodist."

"Well, that's an advantage for the Methodists. Orion's a tireless church worker, so every time he switches religions, the members of his new faith are glad to get him."

"That's a fact," Jane said, tamping the pipe with a thumb. "What's your religion, Sam? Do you go to church regular?"

"Just enough so as not to make a bad habit of it."

She scowled. "I never did understand you when you talk that way. Don't you fear God?"

"Of course I do. You arranged that years ago, when you packed me off to the Hannibal Presbyterian every week. That's where I *learned* to fear God—and dread the Sunday School."

Jane looked at him for a moment, then nodded in satisfaction. "Well, in spite of your flip talk you're a good, righteous man. I know that much from your letters."

"That's because you started me out that way. But how I've happened to stay righteous through the years is a mystery."

She leaned forward. "Maybe it's 'cause I always pray for you, Sam. Every blessed night I get down on my knees and ask the Lord to forgive you for your sins."

"I appreciate that, Ma. But while I don't mean to belittle your efforts to whitewash me, I believe you'd pray for *any* sinner—even Satan himself."

"Of course, why wouldn't I pray for Satan? After all, he's the one sinner that needs it most."

Laughing, Sam pulled over his valise and opened it. "Mrs. Clemens, you deserve a reward for that remark. It was worth at least ten dollars, but you'll have to settle for something that fetches only a dollar and a quarter." He took a small blue and gold volume from the valise. "Here, Ma, with the compliments of the author."

Jane was delighted. "Sammy—is this the book you wrote me everybody's so excited about?"

"Yep, this is it. It's not in the same class with the Holy Scriptures, but I like to think of it privately as 'The First Book of Samuel.'"

She read the title aloud: "'The Celebrated Jumping Frog of Calaveras County,' by Mark Twain. Thank you, son. I'll always treasure this." She opened the cover. "I see you wrote some words here in the front."

"Yep, so I did."

She read the inscription: "'For my mother—but for whose continuous collaboration over three quarters of a year, the Clemens family would have been smaller by one. Lovingly, Sam.' That's real nice, Sammy," she said seriously, "but not exactly the truth. I only carried you for seven months."

"I forgot that. If I ever have another book to inscribe to you, I'll make the correction."

Jane riffled the pages uneasily. "There's no bad words in here, are there?"

"Nope," he replied, pointing heavenward, "that book wouldn't even cause a blush up yonder."

"Sam!" she said severely. "Don't joke about heaven."

"I didn't mean to, Ma."

"Well, don't." She studied him for a moment. "Tell me somethin' truthfully—do you still swear as much as you used to?"

19

"Not by half. These days I only cuss under pressure."

"I'm glad to hear it. You used to near break my heart with your nasty language." She leaned forward and patted his hand. "Excuse me, son. I don't mean to rant at you on your first night here." She closed the book. "I'll read this later when I'm alone. Right now I want to talk. What're you plannin' to do? You goin' to stay here a while?"

"A day or two, if you'll have me."

"You could stay forever if you'd a mind to."

"Thanks, but I'm leaving the country shortly, and there's a mountain of work to do beforehand."

"You wrote me you were thinkin' of goin' around the world."

"Yes, but I've given that up for a trip that's a hundred times better." Excitement crept into his voice. "Ma, month after next I'm sailing away on the most prodigious ocean voyage since Noah's."

"Where to?"

"Europe and the Holy Land."

"The *Holy* Land?" Her jaw dropped in disbelief. "Sam, are you humbuggin' me?"

"No, Ma, it's a fact. On the eighth of June the steamship *Quaker City* leaves New York for a whole summer's journeying to the shores of the Mediterranean."

Sam had seen the announcement of the *Quaker City* excursion several weeks earlier, and the idea had fascinated him. Nothing like it had ever been attempted before—a five-month cruise to romantic lands in the

20

company of refined intellectuals. The advertisement listed Henry Ward Beecher, the prominent Brooklyn clergyman, among the passengers, as well as General Sherman and a host of ministers and journalists. Visualizing an exciting, salaried holiday, Sam had persuaded a newspaper, the *Alta California,* to pay twelve hundred and fifty dollars for his passage and send him along as its special correspondent. Throughout the trip he was to mail back a series of travel letters at the rate of twenty dollars each.

"The sailing's almost two months off," he told his mother, "but I'm in a fever to get away. It's going to be a splendid picnic."

Jane scowled. "A picnic? In the Holy Land?"

"All right, an adventure, if that sounds better. And a paid one at that. How's that for a stroke of luck?"

"It's just grand, Sammy. I'm real happy for you. But even though I don't lay eyes on you for years on end, I'm goin' to miss you. And bein' so far away on an ocean trip like that, I'll worry about you, too."

"You won't have to fear for my safety, Ma. The *Quaker City*'s a fine, seaworthy vessel."

Jane's eyes twinkled. "Oh, I'm not worried about you drownin', Sam. Like I always say—people born to be hanged are safe on water."

2

EARLY one evening in June, in the home of a family that Mark Twain had never heard of, in a city where he had never set foot, baggage was being packed for the ocean voyage to Europe and the Holy Land aboard the steamship *Quaker City*.

The drawing room of the Langdon mansion in Elmira, New York, had a somber aspect, in keeping with the grim tastes of "The Brown Period." The heavily curtained windows and deeply upholstered furniture, the costly but traditional oils and statuettes, gave the impression of conservatism backed by solid wealth. The wealth had been accumulated by the master of the house, Jervis Langdon, through the ownership of mines and shrewd dealings in iron and coal.

Although Langdon was socially a liberal, having been a prewar abolitionist and active in the Underground Railway, he was a Congregationalist devoted to prayers and Bible reading and strongly opposed to the use of alcohol, tobacco, and strong language.

His family consisted of his wife Olivia, their daughter Livy, twenty-one, and their son Charles, a rather undisciplined lad of eighteen. It was Charlie who was being sent on the transatlantic journey, as such trips were considered the civilized way of polishing the rough edges of a boy in his teens.

At the foot of the mahogany staircase that swept upward to wide corridors and countless rooms, Charlie's two carelessly packed valises lay open on a tapestried piano bench. A steamer trunk stood nearby, its lid thrown back to reveal rumpled clothing. A gummed label on the side of the trunk bore the legend:

HOLY LAND

PLEASURE EXCURSION

S.S. "QUAKER CITY"

For the better part of an hour, Olivia Langdon had been dashing upstairs and down, bringing her son clothing she fancied he would need and observing his clumsy packing with nervous disapproval. As the hour of his departure drew near, she grew increasingly apprehensive. A sudden inspiration took her out to the dining room, from which she returned with a cut-glass tumbler. "Charles dear," she announced, "I want you to pack this very, very carefully. It's quite a nice piece of —" Realizing that the boy had vanished, she called out fretfully, "Charles? Charles, where are you?" In exasperation she nearly screamed the name: *"Charles!"*

The door of the study beside the staircase burst

open, and her husband appeared, carrying a sheaf of business correspondence. With his shock of dark hair and black Dickensian beard, Jervis Langdon cut a commanding figure. "What is it, my dear?" he asked anxiously. "Anything wrong?"

"Why must he always be running off?" Olivia cried. "Where has he gone now?"

"Who, Barney?"

"No, *Charles!*"

He patted her arm to lessen her agitation. "I have no idea, Olivia. Now suppose you sit down and rest and I'll find him."

She flung an arm out toward the open luggage. "And look at this horrible disorder. He's just thrown his clothing in." Picking up a rumpled shirt, she attempted to fold it with trembling hands.

With a sigh Jervis put down his letters and gently took the shirt from her. "Please, my dear, the boy must learn to do these things himself. And I'll see that he does." His voice boomed up the staircase: "Charlie! Where are you?"

"In my room, Father."

"Come down here at once!"

"Yes, sir." Charlie came racing down the staircase, trailing a necktie. "What is it?" he asked timidly.

"Charlie, your mother has had quite enough to do getting you ready to leave. Now I want you to get busy and repack your clothing, neatly and properly." Leading Charlie to the trunk, he handed him the rumpled shirt. "Here, start with this."

Charlie bit his lip. "But—well all right, Father, I'll try."

"What's the trouble?" Langdon asked as Charlie wrestled awkwardly with the shirt.

"I'm not used to doing things like this, Father."

"Then you'd better learn in a hurry. Nobody's going to do it for you on the boat."

"No, sir, I guess not."

His father spoke in a low tone. "Calm down, son. After tonight you'll be on your own for five whole months."

Charlie smiled wanly. "Yes, sir."

His mother approached and handed him the cut-glass tumbler. "Here, Charles, pack this in a good safe place."

He frowned. "A drinking glass?"

"A *clean* drinking glass. I want you to use it everywhere you go—especially in France."

"But, Mother, I—" He glanced at his father, who winked and nodded. "Oh, all right, Mother—thanks."

"Now, Olivia," said her husband, "while Charlie's finishing up, why don't you come into my study and lie down?"

"Later, Jervis." She hurried up the stairs. "Charles, I'm going to your room just once more, to make sure you'll have everything you'll need."

"But, Mother," he called after her, "I've already got twice as much as I'll ever need."

His father raised a silencing hand. "You might as well surrender, son. You know your mother."

"Yes, sir, I sure do." Lifting the top layer of clothing, he tossed the tumbler into the trunk.

As he was staring at the open valises, the front door opened and a hulking, red-haired man entered. He was the Langdons' coachman and man of all work, an affable Irishman named Barney.

"The wagon's in the driveway, Charlie," he boomed. "Trunk ready to go yet?"

"Not nearly," Charlie replied dolefully. "Father says all this stuff's got to be packed over again."

Langdon picked up his letters. "Give the boy some help, will you, Barney?"

Barney touched his forehead with a finger. "Sure thing, Mr. Langdon. I'm an old hand at this kind of business."

Jervis walked to the study, consulting his pocket watch. "Don't dally now, son. The New York sleeper leaves the depot in exactly one hour and thirty-two minutes."

"I'll be ready in plenty of time," Charlie assured him.

"Well now, Charlie me boy, let's get to it," Barney said, digging into one of the valises. "Holy Hannah! Looks like you bought out every haberdashery store in town."

Charlie snorted. "I won't need half the junk Mother's making me take." He lifted an armload of clothes. "Look at this, Barney—all my heavy woolen suits. Where I'm going it'll be hot as hell, dammit!"

Barney shot a glance toward the study and laughed. "And hell's just what they'll give you if they catch you usin' them cuss words." He stepped back, hands on hips. "Charlie, I can't get it through me head they're leavin' you break away like this all by yourself."

"Neither can I, but they think it's part of my education. I'm supposed to come back from Europe stuffed with culture or something."

"Well, a bit of learnin' won't do you no harm, I guess." Nudging Charlie with his elbow, he spoke from the side of his mouth. "But don't forget to have yourself a bit of fun on the side."

"Ha, fat chance. I've seen the passenger list, and a lot of them are ministers and missionaries."

"That's a pity. And all Presbyterians, I wouldn't doubt."

Charlie brightened. "But they're not all religious people." He lowered his voice. "Barney, have you ever heard of Mark Twain?"

Barney's eyes widened. "Mark *Twain?*"

"Sh, not so loud."

"Mark Twain?"

"You've heard of him?"

"Sure, who ain't? That jumpin' frog feller. Is *he* gonna be on the boat?"

"Yes, but my parents don't know it, so for heaven's sake don't mention his name."

"Why not, Charlie? Is he a boozer?"

Charlie shrugged. "Well—he's kind of different from

27

the people we know in Elmira. Father may not mind, but Mother wouldn't approve of him, I'm sure."

"You can bet not. But I got an idea he's my kind of man. I'd sure like to meet him."

Charlie straightened his shoulders. "I *intend* to meet him, Barney, first thing."

As the valises were being closed, Olivia came down, carrying an armload of heavy clothing. Barney hurried to assist her. "Here, Mrs. Langdon, let me take that load."

"Thank you, Barney. Be sure to pack them neatly, Charles."

"But, Mother," Charlie complained, "the valises are already closed up tight."

"Then put them in the trunk. On cold, rainy days at sea you'll bless me for my forethought." Olivia hurried back up the stairs. "I'll be right back. I just want to see if there's anything we forgot."

Charlie made a helpless gesture. Barney waited until Mrs. Langdon had disappeared, then picked up the valises and the pile of clothing and took them to the front door. I'll hide these duds in my own closet till you get back, Charlie."

Charlie held the door open. "Thanks, you're a brick. I guess you can come back for the trunk in about five minutes." Closing the door, he stared helplessly at the trunk. In a moment his father came from the study, carrying a handsome rolled umbrella.

"Charlie," he said, "I've decided to lend you this."

"But, *Father*—"

"Take good care of it, son. It's the good one I keep for church."

"But, Father, an umbrella—on a *boat?*"

Jervis hooked the umbrella onto the trunk. "Don't fuss—just take it. Where has your mother gone?"

"Upstairs—to bring down more junk I won't need."

"I know how you feel, son, but please take the things without argument. She loves you with all her heart."

"I know that, Father, and—thanks for the umbrella."

The door opened quietly and Livy Langdon entered, carrying an armful of roses. Charlie's sister was a frail person, unworldly and altogether lovely. Her jet black hair, worn straight back, accentuated the ivory paleness of her skin.

"Oh, Charlie," Livy said forlornly, "Barney told me you're almost ready to leave."

"That's right, almost."

"Oh dear, I can hardly bear it. We're really going to lose you."

"But, Livy sweetheart," her father said, "he'll only be gone five months."

"I know, Father, but it will seem much longer."

While Livy was placing the roses in a vase, Olivia came down with several more odd items for Charlie. "Now, Charles," she announced, "at last you have everything you are going to need."

"I'm sure of that, Mother." With his father's help he began tucking the things into the corners of the trunk.

Olivia glanced at her daughter and shook her head. "Livy dear, were you out in the night air without a shawl?"

A shadow crossed Livy's face. "I was warm enough, Mother. It's a lovely evening."

"But you know how delicate you are, darling. You just cannot afford to take chances with your health."

"I know that, Mother," the girl said patiently.

Six years earlier, Livy had become an invalid, owing to a fall while ice skating. For two years she had been kept in bed, forced to lie virtually motionless. Following treatment by a number of eminent medical men, she regained mobility at last and was able to lead a fairly normal but sheltered life. Her parents and brother idolized her, but having been warned that she would never be robust, their solicitude was so intense that even the girl herself was convinced that she was delicate and could never look forward to a "healthy" marriage.

"Charles, you speak to your sister about taking care of herself," Olivia directed. "She listens to you."

Charlie took Livy's hand and led her across the room. "You will take care of yourself while I'm away, won't you, sis?"

"Of course I will."

"When I get back, I want you to feel just great. I expect your cheeks to look just like those roses."

"They will, I promise." She pressed his arm. "Oh, Charlie, I'm going to miss you terribly. Will you write to me?"

"From every port in the Mediterranean."

Livy drew him to a table filled with family photographs. "Well, just so you won't forget, I'll give you a little reminder to take with you." She handed him a miniature portrait in a hinged case of purple velvet. "Here—my plain little face. Will you keep it in your cabin?"

"No, in my pocket."

"And remember," Livy directed, "whenever you look at my portrait, it will be saying, 'Charlie Langdon, please sit down and write me a long letter.' "

He patted her cheek. "I will, sis, don't worry." Closing the case, he put it in his breast pocket.

Mr. Langdon fastened the hasps of the trunk and locked it. "There, it's ready to go." He handed the key to Charlie. "Here, put this on your key ring and don't lose it."

"Don't worry, sir, I won't."

"It's going to be a great adventure, son. I'd like to have had this chance to travel when I was your age. I really envy you."

"So do I," Livy said. "I wish I were going with you, Charlie."

Mrs. Langdon smoothed Livy's hair. "Don't fret, darling. You and I will have a lovely time all summer, sitting in the garden."

"Yes, while Charlie's traveling," Livy said wanly. "How exciting!"

"But, Livy dear—Charles is a boy."

"How lucky for him! Sometimes I can't help wishing

31

that God had changed his mind and made me a boy."

"Livy!" her mother exclaimed, truly shocked.

"But I mean it. Must I spend my entire life just sitting in the garden?"

Jervis slipped his arm around her waist, speaking tenderly. "Be patient, sweetheart. Some day, when you're stronger, perhaps you and I will see the world together." With a sidelong glance at Olivia he added hastily, "Along with your mother, naturally."

"Oh, I do hope so, Father."

Barney entered from the driveway. "Excuse me. I come for the trunk. Is it ready to go now?"

"It sure is," Charlie answered. "Take it away."

Barney unhooked the umbrella from the trunk and laughed. "Hey, Charlie, you're gonna look like a regular dandy when you get on the boat with this. If Mark Twain sees it, I bet he'll whoop."

"Barney!" Charlie warned.

Barney tossed him the umbrella. "Sorry, Charlie, it slipped out." Loading the trunk onto his back, he carried it outside. "The wagon's ready whenever you are," he shouted.

"Charles," his mother said accusingly, "what did Barney mean? Is that man really going to be on the boat with you?"

Charlie stared down at his feet. "Yes, Mother."

"Oh, my gracious." She made a helpless gesture toward her husband.

"Now, my dear, don't upset yourself," Jervis said.

"I've heard that Mark Twain is a most attractive individual."

"Attractive? A man who's known as the 'Wild Humorist of the Pacific Slope'—attractive?"

"Well, that's what I've heard."

"Jervis, did you know he was going to be one of the passengers?"

He nodded. "Yes, Olivia, I did."

"Then why didn't—"

"I didn't tell you because I knew it would upset you, that's all. Truthfully, I don't think Charlie will be the least bit harmed by the man."

Livy had been listening, completely baffled. "But who is he?" she asked. "I've never even heard of him."

"I should hope not," her mother said. "Charles, I can't begin to tell you how this news distresses me. I've read that Mark Twain is not only a freethinker, but that he swears, smokes, and drinks—constantly."

"Well, maybe so, Mother. But I don't think he'll do much of that on the *Quaker City*. There are sixty-seven passengers, and a whole bunch of them are churchmen."

Olivia seemed slightly mollified. "Well, if he should ever try to speak to you, Charles, you just turn around and walk away."

Langdon looked at his watch and started out the door. "Come on, son, time's getting short. If you miss the train, the boat isn't going to wait for you tomorrow."

"We'll all come out and wave good-bye to you," Livy said.

"No, dear," said her mother, "you're to stay in out of the night air and wave from the window."

"Oh, Charlie," Livy moaned, after her mother had gone, "isn't this awful?"

"But she's right you know, sis. You've really got to take care of your health." He kissed her cheek. "Good-bye, sis, have a good summer."

"Good-bye." She clutched his arm as he was starting out. "Wait—before you go."

"Yes?"

"Tell me something. Who is this what's-his-name that Mother thinks is so wicked?"

Charlie's face lit up. "Mark Twain? Only one of the most popular men in the U.S.A., that's all." He glanced at the door and lowered his voice. "Don't dare tell Mother, but my cabin's number eleven, right next to *his.*"

Livy giggled. "No! Really?"

"Absolutely. In my first letter I'll tell you all about him."

"Please do, Charlie, don't you dare forget. . . . Oh, listen—you'd better address it in care of Barney—so Mother won't read it and have fits."

"I'll do that. 'Bye, sis."

Blowing Livy a kiss, he hurried out to the wagon.

3

IN St. Louis Mark had told his mother that his lecture scheduled for New York City scared him "a little," but as the May 6 date approached, his anxiety mounted until it reached the cold-sweat stage. The lecture had been suggested and arranged by Frank Fuller, who had known and admired Mark in the West. Declaring that a New York appearance would establish Mark's reputation on the East Coast, Fuller had engaged the largest lecture hall available, Cooper Union.

One look at the cavernous auditorium convinced Mark that he would be addressing more empty seats than customers, but Fuller assured him that he would be a resounding success and publicized the event with his customary enthusiasm. The lecture was entitled: "Kanakadom, or the Sandwich Islands," tickets fifty cents. "The Wisdom will begin to flow at 8," Mark added to the printed announcement.

Handbills were distributed in horsecars, hotels, and other public places, but to Mark's dismay few citizens seemed sufficiently interested even to pick them up and read them. By May 1, when only a dozen tickets had been sold, he was panicked. "Nobody's going to be in that hall but you and me," he told Fuller. "Unless you want my suicide on your conscience, you'd better paper the house. Send free tickets everywhere. Drop them out of balloons—even give them to preachers if you have to —but don't make me tell jokes to two thousand empty seats that can't laugh or applaud."

Acting upon Mark's suggestion, Fuller guaranteed him the most intelligent audience ever assembled, and sent floods of complimentary tickets to all the school-teachers of New York, Brooklyn, and adjacent localities.

On the evening of the lecture Mark was still convinced that he was about to make an enormous fool of himself by addressing an empty hall. But when his carriage drew near Cooper Union, he found the entire neighborhood blocked with crowds of people, all trying to get inside. When he finally reached the platform and looked out at a packed house, he was so relieved and elated that he kept his audience laughing for an hour and fifteen minutes.

The next day the newspaper reports were glowing; congratulations came to Mark from all sides, and his fame was assured. Offers to lecture came as well, but he could not accept them, for the date of the *Quaker City* sailing, the eighth of June, was only a month away.

"I am wild with impatience to move," he wrote his mother. " . . . and so I say good-by and God bless you

—and welcome the wind that wafts a weary soul to the sunny lands of the Mediterranean."

The *Quaker City* was a satisfactory ship for her time. Registered at eighteen hundred tons, she could make ten knots under steam, aided when necessary by auxiliary sails.

By noon on sailing day many of the passengers had already come aboard her, at her Wall Street pier. Henry Ward Beecher and General Sherman were not to make the journey, however, both having canceled their reservations, to the heavy disappointment of the others.

Although most of the sixty-seven passengers were middle-aged, pious, and opulent, there were exceptions whom Mark Twain was to find congenial throughout the voyage. Among them were Dan Slote, a stout, balding chap from Brooklyn; Jack Van Nostrand, a fun-loving citizen of Greenville, New Jersey; and the ship's surgeon from Stroudsburg, Pennsylvania, Dr. A. Reeves Jackson.

Dan Slote had boarded the ship early in the morning. After unpacking he made his way up to the main deck, where he could observe the arrival of carriages bringing other passengers, and the noisy bustle of preparations for the scheduled sailing at two in the afternoon.

Several hours later Jack Van Nostrand arrived, checked into his quarters, and came topside. After he and Dan had made themselves known to each other,

Jack leaned on the railing watching the activity on the pier, while Dan sank into a deck chair.

"I wonder if we'll have any shipboard romances," Jack said.

"You'd better think of something else," Dan advised. "We're not going to see one good-looking female until we go ashore in France."

Jack turned, frowning. "How can you be so sure?"

"From what I've already observed. I got on this ark at nine this morning and watched the gangplank for an hour. You should have seen what lumbered up, two by two. The females, Jack, if indeed that's what they were, all looked like elephants, crows, or water spaniels."

Jack glanced down at the pier. "Here comes a pair that look like anteaters." He shuddered. "I'm afraid you're right, Dan. This trip's going to be a washout."

Dan stared at the awning above his head. "I told my old man I didn't want to leave home this summer, but he insisted. When we get to Africa, I think I'll mail him a shrunken head."

Jack brightened. "Well, anyway, Mark Twain should take the curse off of it—if he ever gets here."

"Right you are," Dan said. "I just hope he doesn't get drunk and miss the boat."

Jack indicated a man in uniform who was making his way along the deck. "Here comes an officer. Maybe he knows something."

"Excuse me, sir," Dan said respectfully. "Are you the captain?"

The officer grinned. "No, Captain Duncan wears four stripes. I'm Reeves Jackson, the ship's surgeon."

Dr. Jackson was a tall, spare, chestnut-haired man of thirty-five, with a professional bearing, a genial smile, and a friendly manner. Dan and Jack introduced themselves and told him they were looking for Mark Twain.

"He hasn't come aboard yet to my knowledge," Jackson told them. "Are you men friends of his?"

"No, Doc, but we're anxious to meet him," Dan said.

"So am I. I'm a Twain enthusiast myself."

During the conversation Charlie Langdon had come aboard, staggering under the burden of his valises and umbrella. Wandering along the murky corridors in search of his cabin, he lost his way. Emerging finally into the "grand saloon," he kicked open a door and found himself on the deck just behind Dan, Jack, and the doctor. As the door swung shut, they turned and beheld a travel-worn young man, looking miserably confused.

At the sight of the uniform Charlie's face lit up. "Oh, excuse me, sir. I was looking for cabin eleven, but I got lost."

"You're found now," Jackson said pleasantly.

"Holy smokes!" Jack roared. "Look what's hooked on his arm—an umbrella."

Charlie attempted to hide the umbrella behind his back, but Jack grabbed it and held it aloft. "Hey, give me that!" Charlie cried.

"What's the idea of bringing a bumbershoot?" Dan

asked. "You expect this boat to leak from the top?"

"My father made me bring it," Charlie said unhappily.

"His papa made him bring it," Jack taunted. "Isn't that sweet?"

Dr. Jackson snatched the umbrella from Jack and tossed it back to Charlie. "Here, young fellow, don't let these ruffians get your goat. They probably never had fathers—that they could locate."

Dan and Jack laughed good-naturedly. The doctor shook Charlie's hand. "Welcome aboard. I'm Reeves Jackson, the doctor."

Charlie was relieved to have found a sympathetic shipmate. "Thank you, sir. My name's Charlie Langdon. Say, maybe you can tell me something—has Mark Twain gotten here yet?"

"I don't think so." The doctor seemed impressed. "Do you know Mark Twain?"

"Not yet, but I want to meet him just as soon as I can."

"Well, join the posse, pardner," Dan said. "*All* of us are hunting for Mark Twain."

"I heard that," came a drawling voice from the saloon door. "You fellows make me sound like a horse-thief."

As the four men looked around, Mark stepped out onto the deck. He was smoking a huge cigar and carrying a thick, rolled umbrella.

"It's him!" Jack cried.

"Well I'll be damned," exclaimed Dan.

Mark glared at the group from beneath his shaggy brows. "If this is a hanging party, I plead innocent." Greeting him noisily, they stumbled over each other's feet to clap him on the back. "Well now," Mark said finally, "that was a mighty flattering welcome, and I'm pleased you all hold me in such high esteem." He inhaled his cigar and blew out a dense cloud. "I only hope you'll remember to be this friendly if we ever have to race each other for the lifeboats."

The doctor pumped Mark's hand. "Mr. Twain, I'm Reeves Jackson, doctor on duty. Welcome to the *Quaker City.*"

"Thank you, Doctor, I'm pleased to be aboard." He pointed eastward. "I haven't met your captain yet, but in case he doesn't know, tell him Europe lies over in that general direction."

"Captain Duncan's already made sure of that—at least I hope he has."

"And don't you fall overboard, Doctor, whatever you do. I just walked through the ship's kitchen, and by the looks of it we're all going to need your services right after dinner."

Jackson laughed. "How did you manage to get aboard without our seeing you?"

"I sneaked up the crew's gangplank—an old habit of mine." Mark glanced at the others. "Now that I know the doctor, let me get you fellows straight."

Jack put his hand out. "I'm Jack Van Nostrand."

"A pleasure, Jack."

Dan stepped forward. "I'm Dan Slote, and I'm afraid I've got bad news for you."

Mark frowned. "You're a Baptist preacher?"

"No, but you're stuck with me as a cabin-mate. Do you mind?"

"Hell no, Dan. I can outsnore any man that ever slept with his mouth open." Mark looked at Charlie, who had been hanging back shyly. "*You* don't look like a Baptist."

"No, sir, I'm a Congregationalist."

Mark looked sympathetic. "Well, we're all afflicted in different ways. Now tell me your name."

"Charlie Langdon, sir—from Elmira, New York." He grinned and pointed to Mark's umbrella. "I'm glad to see you brought one, too."

"Oh sure, Charlie, I always carry this old umbrella— hoping for a chance to swap it for a better one."

"Just before you came, these fellows were ragging me about bringing mine."

"Well, that's only natural I guess. But you and I will have the last laugh when we're parading in that damned Egyptian sun." Mark put a hand to his mouth. "Oh, excuse my language—I forgot you were Congregationalist."

"That's all right." Charlie grinned. "I didn't mind it a damned bit."

Mark's eyebrows shot up. "Hear that, fellows? This Congregationalist is almost cured."

"If he keeps improving," Dan said, "he might become a hardened sinner like the rest of us. There aren't many of us on this tub, Mark."

"Yes, I noticed that just now when I passed through the public saloon here. Come have a look." He stepped to the door and opened it. "If you men aren't afraid of getting seasick before we get under way, step inside with me and see a cross section of our traveling companions."

Inside the saloon, groups of passengers, some with visitors who had come to bid them bon voyage, milled about or sat on plush-covered lounges consulting maps and guidebooks. A number of them made ostentatious displays of Bibles, prayerbooks, and the Plymouth Collection of Hymns. Most of them were dressed in dark-colored costumes, giving them the cheerless appearance of ravens.

Mark studied the scene for a moment, then turned to Reeves Jackson. "Doctor, it appears to me that your ship will be carrying a cargo of venerable fossils, most of them fired up with professional piety."

Reeves nodded. "Well, churchmen aren't such a bad lot, once you get to know them."

"You've got a point there," Mark admitted. "To be truthful, I'm right fond of preachers. If they're not narrow-minded and bigoted, they make good companions."

Dan gave a snort. "I'm just afraid that the 'venerable fossils' are going to turn this boat party into a prayer meeting."

"I don't mind prayer meetings," Mark said, "if I can sneak away once an hour and smoke a cigar." He headed for the door. "Come on, it's time to sneak."

Back on deck again, he opened a cigar case, took out a fresh one, and passed the case around. "Here you are, boys. Fire up and enjoy yourselves." While all save Charlie were lighting up, he observed with a drawl, "I didn't expect to find this little pocket of human beings on the boat. It proves an old theory of mine: when you're expecting the worst, you get something that's not so bad after all."

The door of the grand saloon burst open, and a squat, rotund man in a suit of clothes-closet green waddled out, sniffing the air. Spotting the smokers, he stopped short, bristling with disapproval. "Well! At last I've discovered the source of the abomination."

"If you're the captain," Dan said severely, "you're out of uniform."

"I am not the captain," the man protested. "I am Deacon William F. Church. These filthy cigars—their sickening stench has permeated the grand saloon. As a clergyman I insist that you men put them out at once."

"As a citizen," Mark said, "I insist that you read the Bill of Rights."

The little man stared up at Mark and gave a sudden gasp of recognition. "Aha!" he exclaimed, wagging a finger under Mark's moustache. "Now I know who you are—you're Mark Twain! I demand that you put out that disgusting cigar."

44

"Oh dear," Mark said with a sigh. "Oh dear, oh dear. Reverend, a minute ago I had a good word to say for certain members of your profession. Why did you have to come along and make me out a damned liar?"

As the others burst into laughter, Deacon Church recoiled as if from the devil, backed up to the door, and vanished into the saloon.

"Good work, Mark," Jack said. "You sure told that old buzzard off."

Mark shrugged. "It was a waste of breath."

"But you were great," Dan insisted. "I bet you made him wish he'd missed the boat."

Mark shook his head sadly. "Whenever I see Mankind fallen that low, it seems a pity that Noah and his party didn't miss *their* boat." He contemplated his dead cigar. "Somebody give me a light. That cold-hearted cuss put my fire out."

When the *Quaker City* passed through the Narrows into the open sea, the first transatlantic pleasure cruise was under way. No land would be seen until they approached the Azores eleven days later.

For the duration of the five-month journey, Mark, Dan, Jack, and the doctor clung together, a small fraternity of dissidents resisting the intolerant respectability of the pilgrims. In time Charlie Langdon, now called "the cub," was accepted as a member of the inner circle, despite his ingenuousness and lack of years.

45

4

WHEN the *Quaker City* arrived at the Holy Land, Mark and a group went ashore at Beirut for a month's camping trip on horseback to Jerusalem. His traveling companions, as usual, were Dan, Jack, and Charlie, and, almost inconceivably, Deacon Church, the disapprover of cigars, alcohol, and Mark Twain.

In the parched hills of Palestine the heat made the discomfort difficult to bear, and none of the party save the deacon felt particularly fit. All day long they rode gaunt horses in single file, each man except Mark protected from the scorching sun by enormous spectacles equipped with green glass, a gigantic white umbrella lined with green, and a red fez with the white rag of Constantinople wound around it and dangling down the back.

One morning before daylight the travelers were dressing inside a pair of striped tents pitched among sere trees and crumbling walls near the ruins of Jericho. A short distance away a ragged native dragoman was scratching himself and packing his saddlebag. Ferguson, as he was dubbed by the members of the party, was their guide and interpreter.

At dawn, when the first shaft of brassy sunlight lanced the dusty gloom, Ferguson clanged a handbell, intoning in a reedy, irritating voice: "Hello, everybody! The morning comes! Daylight is with us!"

"Shut up, Ferguson, for God's sake!" Dan bellowed from his tent.

"All people get ready to come out quick!" Ferguson continued. "I saddle horses in ten minutes! Soon we eat breakfast on shore of River Jordan!"

"To hell with the River Jordan!" Jack yelled.

"Today," Ferguson went on, "all take boat ride on Dead Sea!"

"The Dead Sea," Dan repeated in disgust. "That's what I wish *I* was—dead."

Deacon Church emerged from his tent, costumed outlandishly for the day's journey. "Ah, the Dead Sea," he exclaimed joyously to Ferguson. "Those eternally blessed waters."

"Huh?" said Ferguson blankly.

Jack, also dressed in absurd traveling gear, came through the tent flap, grunting. "What're you so excited about, Deacon?"

"This wondrous day and all it is about to bring. This is the day I've dreamt of all my life. At last I shall glimpse the blessed waters that cover wicked Sodom and Gomorrah. And beyond," the Deacon continued, flinging his arm out, "are the Mountains of Moab, where Moses lies buried."

Jack frowned. "Moses who?"

Deacon Church looked pained. "Really, Jack, your flippant attitude about the Holy Land distresses me more than I can say. I hope you will be properly respectful when we arrive at the Dead Sea."

"Maybe," said Jack, "but I bet it'll cost us a fortune to rent a boat." He called to Ferguson. "Hey, Fergy, how much will they charge us to rent a boat at the Dead Sea?"

"Two Napoleon—eight dollar."

Jack's jaw dropped. "The damned robbers. That's what they soaked us to cross the Sea of Galilee. No wonder Christ walked."

Deacon Church looked heavenward. "Oh, Jack, Jack, your blasphemy is sinful. I think you've been associating too closely with"—he lowered his voice—"a certain person who shares your tent."

"Mark?"

"Of course. His behavior all through the Holy Land has been disgraceful. Bursting into tears at the tomb of Adam—now *really*."

"But he was deeply touched," Jack said with a straight face. "Don't you realize that? He said it was the grave of a distant blood relation."

"A scandalous remark. He's a sinful man, Jack."

Jack bridled. "I'll argue that," he said hotly. "Was he sinful when he stayed behind with Dan when Dan had cholera?"

"No, that was a truly Christian act."

"And in spite of that you still don't approve of him?"

The deacon made a helpless gesture. "As a church-man, how can I approve of him? He's not only sinful—he's irreverent and profane. Mark Twain, my dear Jack, is the worst man I've ever known."

"Now wait just a—"

"And one of the very best," Deacon Church added with deep sincerity.

Ferguson buckled his saddlebag and went off to water the horses. In a moment Dan Slote and Charlie Langdon stepped from their tent, grotesquely costumed and equipped for the day's trip. Dan's umbrella was the tourist's standard white and green model; Charlie's was his father's black Sunday best, already looking gray and shabby.

Dan was talking bitterly, to no one in particular. "I don't know whether I can face another day of this rotten pilgrimage. I think I'll gallop down to the Jordan and drown myself."

"Go ahead," Jack said. "When I get home and tell your parents you went to glory in holy water, they'll be overcome with religious fervor."

Charlie fanned himself with his fez. "This is going to be another scorcher. I'm already exhausted."

"So is Mark," Jack said. "I had to roll him out of his blanket."

"Hey, Mark," Dan yelled, "what's keeping you?"

"Coming, Dan, coming," Mark replied from the tent.

"Look alive, Mark," Deacon Church called brightly. "Look alive."

The tent flap parted and Mark came out, walking

49

stiffly. He was dressed in plain dark clothing and had neither spectacles nor umbrella. "I couldn't look less alive, Deacon," he said, rubbing his seat. "That four-footed hatrack I've been riding every day has numbed my caboose."

Silently, they set to work packing their saddlebags.

"Say, Mark," Charlie said after a moment, "where's your umbrella?"

"In my bedroll, cub, and so are my green spectacles. And if I had a red fez, that would be hidden away, too. I refuse to let myself look as ridiculous as you fellows."

Charlie glanced around the group. "Why do you say that, Mark? I think we look all right."

"Yes, for a masquerade party in Elmira, but not here in ancient Jericho." Mark indicated the crumbling masses of fallen stone. "If Joshua hadn't blown these walls down with his trombone three thousand years ago, you scarecrows would surely have flattened them today."

"Elmira," Charlie said wistfully. "I wonder what my family is doing there right now."

"Probably eating a big chicken dinner with rice and gravy," Dan said.

Turning away from the group, Charlie drew the portrait case from his pocket and glanced furtively at Livy's likeness. Observing the action, Jack waved to get the attention of the others, pointed to Charlie, and pantomimed that he had opened the case.

"Homesick for Elmira, Charlie?" he called in a sing-song voice.

"No!" Red-faced, Charlie thrust the case back into his pocket and resumed his packing.

"The cub's homesick for his girl," Dan said. "The one in that picture he's always mooning over."

"It isn't my girl, it's my sister."

Jack wrinkled his nose. "Your *sister?* God, I can't look at my sister's actual face, let alone her picture."

"She must be a raving beauty, Charlie," Dan teased. "When're you going to let us have a look?"

"Oh, sometime, maybe," Charlie mumbled. "Forget it, will you?"

Deacon Church shouldered his saddlebag and started in the direction of the tethered horses. "Well, I'm ready to proceed," he said. "I'll tell the guide to come and pack the tents. Please don't dally, gentlemen," he called back. "I'm terribly impatient to reach Jordan and the Dead Sea."

Dan called after him. "Better have a salt cellar handy. You might pick up a few grains of Lot's wife."

Jack glanced sideways at Mark. "Who the hell *was* Lot's wife, anyway?"

"Mrs. Lot," Mark explained, "was an over-curious female who ended her days as a pillar of sodium chloride. The local bandits will doubtless charge us four bits apiece to gaze at the spot where her saline solidification took place."

Dan laboriously picked up his saddlebag. "I think I'll stagger down to the clearing and see if my horse is still breathing."

"My nag bit me on the leg yesterday," Jack said. "I

hope the mean bastard has lockjaw." Dragging his bag along the ground, he started off after Dan, calling back, "Mark, are you and the cub about ready to get started?"

"Pretty soon," Mark answered, taking a seat on a time-worn rock. "I always try to delay the agony as long as possible."

"I'll wait and keep Mark company," Charlie shouted, adding to Mark, "You don't mind, do you?"

"Lord no, Charlie, I'm right fond of company when it's not chiseling away at my granite soul."

"I hardly ever get a chance to talk to you without the others around."

"Well, if you like chin-music you've certainly stuck with the right party." Mark peered at Charlie's face. "Say, are you raising a moustache?"

"Trying to," he answered sheepishly, rubbing his upper lip.

"What the devil for?"

"Oh, just for the fun of it, I guess." He indicated Mark's luxuriant growth. "Why did you raise one?"

"Why?" He considered the question for a moment. "I'm hanged if I can remember, Charlie. It was either to impress the girls on the Mississippi or to scare off Indians in Nebraska. As it turned out, it didn't do either one."

Squatting down beside Mark, Charlie asked eagerly, "What was it like on the river? I mean being a steamboat pilot."

A fleeting smile crossed Mark's face. "Well, Charlie,

it gave me as close a look at heaven as I'll ever get." He made a helpless gesture. "I guess that's all I can say about the subject in less than a million words."

"I certainly envy you, Mark. You've seen everything and you've been just about everywhere."

"I haven't been to Elmira, New York."

Charlie shrugged. "But that's nothing. That's where I was brought up."

"The very reason you should hold it in high regard. I was brought up in Hannibal, Missouri, and it always warms me to think back on it."

"I'm sure Hannibal was a lot more exciting than Elmira."

"You might be right at that," Mark said reflectively. "Yep, you just might be right."

Charlie sighed. "I'll be back home in a couple of months, and I'm sure going to miss you, Mark."

"But you'll be with your folks, Charlie—that should please you." Charlie's hand went to his breast pocket, and Mark noticed the gesture. "You seem to have a high regard for your family," he said. He tapped the bulge in Charlie's pocket. "Especially this particular member."

"What?" He colored awkwardly. "Oh, I see what you mean—my sister's picture. Jack and Dan are always teasing me about carrying it."

"But you've teased them even more by not letting them have a look at it. Curiosity's about to kill them both. Why not let them see it?"

"I just don't want to show it around, that's all. I don't think Livy would like it."

"Livy?"

Charlie nodded. "My sister."

"Livy. Hm—a pretty-sounding name."

"It's really Olivia like my mother's, but we always call her Livy. She's really wonderful, Mark."

"You don't say. Pretty?"

"Oh sure, and bright too—just about perfect."

"She sounds almost too good to be human. Is she?"

"Is she what?"

"Human."

Charlie grinned. "Of course."

Mark pondered his next question. "Older than you or younger?"

"Three years older—she's twenty-one."

"Twenty-one—hm. Well, there's only the one obvious question left, so I'll ask it. Is she married?"

"No!" Charlie answered sharply.

Mark's eyebrows shot up. "Well now, in view of the thunder you put behind that 'no,' I've got to ask why not." He bent toward Charlie. "Answer me. Why isn't this paragon married?"

Charlie looked down at his feet. "Well, it's kind of hard to explain. You see, my parents think that—well—to tell you the truth, they think there's no man that's good enough for Livy."

Mark rose to his feet. "Dammit, Charlie, that does it!"

Startled, Charlie jumped up. "Does what?"

"I can't stand this another blasted minute." Mark put his hand out. *"Let me see that portrait!"*

Intimidated by Mark's vehemence, Charlie was about to hand it over when Dan emerged from the clearing. "Hey, come on, will you?" he whined. "It's hot as a pistol out here."

"Right away, Dan," Charlie shouted. With a sidelong glance at Mark, he picked up his saddlebag and started toward the clearing.

Mark gathered his own belongings. "Young whippersnapper," he muttered. "I hope he skewers himself on his old man's umbrella."

One evening at dusk, as the *Quaker City* rolled drowsily in the warm swells of the eastern Mediterranean, Mark stepped into Charlie's cabin in search of a collar button.

"I've got plenty in that drawer," Charlie said. "Help yourself."

"Mine dropped into my soup at dinner," Mark explained, "and I think I swallowed it." As he reached for the collar button, his eyes fell on the portrait case that lay open among Charlie's handkerchiefs.

Charlie heard Mark's sharp intake of breath. "What's the matter?" he asked. "Get a splinter?"

Mark raised the case to the light. "So this is Livy," he murmured.

"What?" Seeing the case, Charlie reached for it, but Mark turned away. Charlie nodded. "Yes, Mark, that's my sister."

"I've never seen the picture of an actual saint," Mark said. "Until—" He stopped short and turned back again. His rugged face softened, and he gazed at the likeness in silent reverence.

"Well?" Charlie asked expectantly. "What do you think of her?"

"God in heaven, Charlie—this girl *is* a saint." Mark's voice fell to a whisper, hoarse with sudden emotion. "So much purity and sweetness and—nobility—in this lovely face. She's—overwhelming." Clearing his throat, he closed the case gently and pressed it tightly between his palms. "Charlie," he said simply, "I want to keep this."

"Oh, no! You can't!" He snatched at the case, but Mark drew his hands back.

"Please, Charlie—I beg you."

Charlie shook his head vehemently. "I'm sorry, Mark. I'd like to, but I just can't. Don't you understand?" Timidly lifting the case from between Mark's reluctant hands, he closed it and returned it to the drawer. "Come on," he said, attempting a smile. "Let's go find Dan and Jack. We'll get a card game going." He stepped out into the corridor and turned. "Coming, Mark?"

Mark's reply was almost inaudible. "Shortly, Charlie, shortly."

A moment later, Mark was standing where Charlie had left him, his palms still pressed tightly together.

5

BY November 19, when the *Quaker City* returned to America, the *Alta California* had published fifty-three of Mark Twain's travel letters and the *New York Tribune* had carried six more. In amazingly colorful and forceful prose, Mark had praised the foreign sights and objects that were honest and forthright and had ridiculed with his abundant store of humor whatever he perceived to be counterfeit. As a result, he arrived in New York with his fame increasing and his literary reputation assured.

Charlie Langdon, like all tourists before and since, had dutifully sent descriptive letters to his family from every port. His private notes to Livy, sent by way of Barney as promised, revealed no more about his relationship with Mark Twain than the fact that they were companionable. The episode of the portrait and Mark's reaction to it had, of course, not been mentioned in any of his family letters.

On the morning of the *Quaker City*'s arrival, Jervis Langdon, in New York on business, took a carriage to the Wall Street pier to welcome Charlie home. When he came aboard the ship, so great was the confusion that he sought a man in officer's uniform to assist him in locating Charlie. Fortunately, the officer he accosted was A. Reeves Jackson, whose duties as ship's surgeon were very nearly concluded. Having introduced himself and learned that the visitor was Charlie Langdon's father, the doctor led him toward that section of the deck where Charlie would most likely be found.

While Jackson and Langdon were making their way through the crowd, Jack Van Nostrand, bundled against the damp morning in a woolen coat and muffler, was impatiently pacing the deck outside the entrance to the cabins. Stopping at the door, he cupped his hands and shouted, "Hey, Dan, are you coming?"

"Right here," came Dan's voice from directly inside. "Hold your horses."

"Get a wiggle on, will you?"

Dan stepped out onto the deck, dropped his valises, and sniffed the air delightedly. "Ah! What's that delicious aroma?"

"That's good old New York air," Jack replied, "so let's get off this tub and enjoy it. What took you so long, Dan? What were you doing in there?"

"Saying adiós to Mark and Charlie."

"Well, let's get down on the pier before the fossils grab all the carriages."

Dan snorted. "The fossils aren't going to *ride* uptown, Jack—they're too damn cheap."

"Well, let's not take any chances. Come on."

While they were hastily assembling their luggage, Reeves Jackson came toward them, followed by Mr. Langdon. "You fellows look like rats leaving a sinking ship," he said. "What's the big hurry?"

"Don't hold us up, Doc," Jack said. "That's civilization out there. I never thought I'd get back to it alive."

"Neither did I," said Dan. "Give the Captain a message for me, will you, Doc? Tell him he can take his rotten Holy Land and—" He stopped short, suddenly aware of Jervis Langdon's stern expression. "I'll be in touch with you, Reeves," he said awkwardly, making his way toward the gangplank.

"Right, Dan," Reeves called after him. "You have my address."

Jack exchanged farewells with Reeves and shuffled after Dan, bent under the weight of his bags and bundles.

Stroking his beard, Jervis looked at the retreating figures. "Some of your pilgrims, Doctor?" he asked quizzically.

"Well yes, Mr. Langdon, in a way," Jackson replied. "Nice chaps. As a matter of fact, your son found them excellent traveling companions."

Jervis raised one eyebrow. "Oh, is that a fact? Hm. I hope I haven't missed the boy."

"I'm fairly sure he hasn't gone ashore yet," Jackson said, "because he promised to look me up and say good-bye. While I look around for him, I suggest you wait inside in the saloon."

"Thank you, Doctor, it is rather brisk out here."

They were approaching the door just as Charlie emerged, struggling with his luggage and umbrella.

"Speak of the devil," Jackson said. "Look here, Charlie, you've got a welcome-home visitor."

Glancing up, Charlie saw his father and exclaimed, "Well, I'll be da—uh—doggoned." Dropping his bags, he shook his father's hand. "Hello, Father. Gosh, this is a surprise!"

"Welcome home, son. We've all missed you."

"If you'll excuse me," the doctor interrupted, "I'll say au revoir to you two Langdons later at the gangplank." With a touch of his cap, he made his way through the chattering throng.

Langdon's attention was drawn to Charlie's upper lip. "Well—I see you've grown a moustache."

"Yes, sir," Charlie said almost apologetically. "Like it?"

"Well—"

"Do you think Mother will mind?"

His father leaned forward for a closer look. "Well, it's a fairly good-sized growth you've got there, but I suppose she'll get used to it after the initial shock." He smiled. "Actually, son, it makes you look older and—uh—rather dignified."

"Really?" Charlie smoothed the moustache, grinning proudly. "Gosh, thanks for saying so. But this is a wonderful surprise, meeting me like this. I had no idea you'd be here."

"I have a business appointment this afternoon," his

father explained. "I invited your mother and Livy to join me on the trip, but your mother didn't want to expose your sister to this damp weather."

"No, sir, I suppose not. How are they, Father?"

"Fine, just fine." Langdon noticed the umbrella on Charlie's arm and winced. "Charlie, is that my—*good* umbrella?"

"Yes, Father," he replied in a small voice, "I'm afraid it is."

Langdon took the umbrella and opened it after a great deal of pushing and tugging. It was faded and bent and ragged around the edges. "What happened to it, Charlie?" he asked plaintively.

"Well, sir, you see it had a lot of wear and tear."

"Obviously." Clucking his tongue, he closed the umbrella and handed it back. "It's yours now, son." He reached for one of Charlie's valises. "Well, let's engage a carriage and drive up to my hotel."

Charlie made a restraining gesture. "Could you wait just one minute, Father? Mark told me he's coming right out, and I'd like you to meet him."

"Mark?"

"Yes, sir, Mark Twain," Charlie said, adding proudly, "I call him Mark and he calls me Charlie."

"You don't say."

"You'll like him, Father," Charlie said defensively, "you really will."

"I'm sure I will, son, if you say so."

"And Livy will, too, even though he's different from

61

anybody we've ever known before. I know you won't believe this, Father, but Mark's just dying to meet Livy."

Langdon scowled. "To meet *Livy?* Why?"

Charlie's face reddened. "Well, he saw my portrait of her one night and thought she was wonderful. He wanted to keep it because he said she was a saint."

"I sincerely hope you didn't let him keep it," his father said sternly.

"Oh no, sir." Charlie tapped his pocket. "It's right here."

"Charlie!" came a voice from inside the door.

"That's Mark!" Charlie said. "I'm out here, Mark!"

Mark's lazy drawl was heard again. "I got waylaid by one of those dadgummed, psalm-singing fossils."

Charlie paled slightly. "See, Father? I told you he's different.

The two Langdons faced the door, and Mark emerged, loaded down with luggage and smoking a huge cigar. "I feel like a damned packhorse, Charlie," he announced without looking up. "If I bust a leg, I might ask you to shoot me."

"Mark!" Charlie warned. "My father's here!"

Mark glanced at Langdon. "Your father?"

"Yes."

"Holy catfish," Mark muttered, dropping everything, including the cigar. To cover his confusion, he added lightly, "Step on that respectfully, will you, Charlie? It's a ten-center."

Charlie ground the cigar under his foot and gestured toward his parent. "This is my father."

"It's a pleasure to meet you, Mr. Langdon," Mark said warmly.

"Delighted, Mr. Twain," Jervis replied unsmilingly. "Or do you prefer Clemens?"

Mark grinned. "It all depends. If you're planning to prosecute me for my language, it's legally Clemens. I apologize for my poor choice of words a moment ago."

"Quite unnecessary. You're well acquainted with the proper ones, I'm sure."

Mark bowed. "Thank you for your confidence."

"Now, Mr. Clemens," Langdon said brusquely, "we'd better not delay you any longer. You have certain professional obligations to attend to, I imagine?"

"Well, yes, Mr. Langdon, I did promise to drop off one travel letter at the *Herald*. But the paper won't collapse if I don't meet my deadline."

Charlie had been eying his father nervously. "Mark read his letters to us almost every night on the boat. They're really great. Have you read them, Father?"

"Of course. They've received wide circulation. They're excellent, Mr. Clemens."

Mark beamed. "Thank you, Mr. Langdon."

"You may not be aware of this, but those letters have increased your reputation enormously."

"I'm pleased to hear that," Mark replied, "but meeting Charlie's father pleases me even more. I must confess I was chary of making your acquaintance, sir, until

Charlie told me you were in the coal business. That relieved me a good deal."

"Relieved you? Why?"

"Well, for some reason I had it in my mind that you were a banker."

Jervis frowned. "And you don't approve of bankers?"

"Not totally. To my mind a banker's a man who lends you an umbrella when the sun's shining and demands it back the minute it starts to rain."

Langdon laughed heartily. "Say, that's good—very good. We'll remember that one, eh, Charlie?"

"Yes," said Charlie, joining in the laughter. "Some of our stuffy Elmira bankers will drop dead in their tracks."

"I didn't say we'll repeat it," his father said soberly. "I merely said we'll remember it."

Charlie flushed. "Oh—yes, sir."

"And now," said Mr. Langdon, picking up one of Charlie's valises, "we really must be going. Good-bye, Mr. Clemens. Good luck to you in your work."

"Thank you, sir. In my line, any amount of luck is appreciated and necessary."

"Don't dally now, Charlie," his father directed, pushing his way through the crowd. "The carriages down on the pier will be at a premium."

Charlie took hold of Mark's hand regretfully. "Well, Mark, I guess this is good-bye. Thanks for being my friend. I certainly hope we'll meet again somewhere."

"Oh, we will, Charlie," Mark assured him. "Maybe in Elmira—who knows?"

Charlie was pleased. "That would be great. Are you planning a trip up our way?"

"Yes, I've been planning it ever since that night I came to your cabin hunting for a collar button."

Charlie looked puzzled, then grinned. "Oh, I see what you mean."

"But it won't be till next summer, I'm afraid."

"Well, whenever it is," Charlie said, "plan to stay at our house as my guest. We've got plenty of rooms."

"Thanks, Charlie. Just one is all I usually need."

Jervis Langdon's voice boomed over the clamor of the passengers and stevedores. "Charlie! Come here at *once!*"

"Right away, Father!" Charlie shouted. Giving Mark a fond pat on the shoulder, he picked up the rest of his luggage and hurried toward the gangplank.

6

MARK TWAIN'S final travel letter, written expressly for the *New York Herald,* was a wickedly satirical lampoon of the *Quaker City*'s Grand Holy Land Pleasure Excursion: "A funeral excursion without a corpse" . . . the daily life on board the ship consisting of "solemnity, decorum, dinner, dominoes, prayer and slander." When the letter appeared in the newspaper, Mark's fellow passengers exploded with indignation; and as if to emulate them, the *Quaker City* herself blew up subsequently and sank off the coast of Bermuda.

The editors of the *Herald* were so well pleased with Mark's letter that they predicted in the same issue of the newspaper that if its author were to write a book based upon his *Quaker City* adventures, it would be unusually successful. On that same day Elisha Bliss, Jr., of the American Publishing Company in Hartford, Connecticut, was struck by the identical thought and wrote Mark suggesting that he compile a book from his letters, with, perhaps, some "interesting additions."

Mark did not receive the Bliss letter immediately, for

after spending only one day in New York, he left for Washington, D.C., to take the post of private secretary to Senator William M. Stewart of Nevada, an odd arrangement from which he soon resigned. The letter from Bliss, which caught up with Mark on December 1, offered him favorable terms for a book and asked him to reply as promptly as possible. He responded the following day, thus beginning one of the most significant author-publisher associations in American letters.

Late in December Mark went to New York to spend the holidays with Dan Slote. The event turned into a *Quaker City* reunion, for they were joined by Jack Van Nostrand and Charlie Langdon. "Those are the best boys in the world," Mark wrote to his mother. "I just laughed till my sides ached at some of our reminiscences."

"The *Quaker City* night-hawks," as they dubbed themselves, tried to outdo each other in irreverence. Dan remarked that the most fun he had had in the Holy Land was when he suffered the attack of cholera. Mark's own joke was even more scathing: "There will be no second advent—Christ having been there once will never come again."

An even more satisfying event for Mark took place several days after Christmas when he at last met Livy Langdon, the saint of the portrait. Charlie, who had been anxious to present his famous friend to his sister, invited him to dine with Livy, Mr. Langdon, and himself at the St. Nicholas Hotel on Lower Broadway.

Mark needed no urging, for he had thought often of the lovely face in the picture and yearned to see the living original.

The Langdons had come down from Elmira to hear Charles Dickens in a reading of his works and, after dinner, invited Mark to accompany them. The party took a carriage to Steinway Hall, where Mark sat beside the Langdons' frail idol while the giant of English literature read passages from *David Copperfield*, *Oliver Twist*, and *Pickwick Papers*.

Returning to the hotel, Mark persuaded Livy to linger over a cup of tea in the public parlor. While he talked, she listened attentively, fascinated by his novel eloquence. When she finally seized an opportunity to speak, she complimented him upon his travel letters.

"Why thank you, Miss Langdon," Mark said. "This is the first time I've ever received honorable mention from an angel."

She stood up. "Now I'm afraid I must say good night, Mr. Clemens. Father is rather strict about my getting sufficient sleep." With a winsome smile she turned to leave.

Mark tugged gently at her arm. "Wait, please."

She turned back eagerly. "Well?"

"Miss Langdon," he began, "or Livy, if you'll allow me that liberty . . ."

"Of course, if you wish."

"Livy then. Livy, may I have your permission to write you from time to time?" Noting her tiny, puzzled frown, he added quickly, "Friendly letters?"

She brightened; she was evidently pleased. "Why, I'd like that very much, Mr.—" She hesitated, unsure.

"Mark?" he prompted her hopefully. "Sam? Whichever you like."

"Mark," she said at once.

Her permission to write elated him, but before he could tell her so, with a shy smile and a fleeting wave of her hand, she was gone.

Watching the tiny figure make its way to the staircase, Mark reached mechanically for a cigar and scratched a match on his trousers. As he brought his hand up, the flame captured his attention, flooding him suddenly with the rapture of reformation. Scornfully, he blew out the match and glared at the cigar with indignation. He was about to toss it into the ashtray when the flood of rapture was stanched by an inbred sense of thrift, and he returned it to his pocket.

To Mark's delight he saw Livy again on New Year's Day, when he and Charlie went on a round of holiday "calls." Again Charlie invited him to come to Elmira for a visit, and although he accepted, many months went by before he appeared as the Langdons' guest. When he set out for Washington, he took with him the memory of Livy's haunting voice and exquisitely fragile beauty.

Early in January, 1868, Mark delivered a Washington lecture entitled "The Frozen Truth," dealing more or less with his *Quaker City* adventures, and several weeks later, in Hartford, he signed a splendid contract with Bliss to write the travel book based upon his *Alta* letters. During the next six months he labored furiously on the manuscript, picking up more than adequate living expenses by writing newspaper articles and delivering lectures throughout the West, traveling as far as San Francisco. During the final week of July he delivered the first draft of his manuscript to Elisha Bliss.

It was not until August, when Mark had freed himself from a mass of burdens and obligations, that he was able to accept Charlie's invitation to visit him and his family in Elmira. Although he had been expected to arrive late in the afternoon, he did not appear until long after dinner, when the Langdons, still seated at the cleared dining table, were being read to by Jervis in accordance with their nightly custom.

Owing either to his impatience to see Mark or his boredom with his father's voice, Charlie finally slipped away into the drawing room, closing the dining room door behind him so as not to have the monologue interrupted by extraneous sounds. Hearing Barney's voice and the sound of carriage wheels in the driveway at last, he called out the door into the darkness, "Mark? Mark, is that you?"

"It's what's left of me," came the familiar drawl, "after the ride up here on that blasted railroad."

Mark climbed the steps from the porte cochere and dropped a scarred valise as he entered the room. "Great to see you, Charlie," he said in a strained voice.

Charlie gasped, noting that Mark resembled a mobile

scarecrow. His face, smudged with coal dust, was sandwiched between a long yellow duster and a wide straw hat with a frayed brim.

"Good grief, Mark!" Charlie exclaimed.

"What's the trouble?"

"What've you got on?"

Mark glanced downward. "My clothes, why?"

"Well—" Charlie made a helpless gesture.

"I always wear *something*," Mark said innocently. "I've discovered that naked people have little or no influence in society."

Charlie closed the door quietly and pointed to Mark's yellow duster. "But what *is* this—thing?"

"This? It's what I call my travel shroud. I've got a dandy suit on under it," he added hastily, "if that's what worries you."

Charlie picked up the valise and drew Mark across the room toward the staircase. "Look, let me take you upstairs before the family sees you."

Mark disengaged his arm. "But shouldn't I be polite and pay my respects?"

Charlie glanced apprehensively at the dining room door. "Later—after you've cleaned up a little."

"Charlie, tell me," Mark said eagerly, "how is Livy?"

"Fine, just tip-top." He jerked Mark's arm impatiently. "Now come on, will you?"

Mark shook free. "But *where* is she?"

"Sh, not so loud." Charlie dropped his voice to a whisper. "She's in the dining room with my parents."

71

"They're having dinner at this hour?"

"No, dinner was over long ago. Father's reading *Bleak House* out loud."

"*Bleak House?*" Mark said incredulously. "God almighty, Charlie, *that's* a damned dismal way to spend an evening."

"Mark, *please* don't swear," Charlie begged. "Not *here,* anyway."

"All right, I'll try not to—but it'll be a hell of an effort."

Charlie cringed and gave Mark a push. "Now come on—let's hurry upstairs."

With Mark in the lead, still clad in his straw hat and duster, they started up the staircase. Midway in their climb the dining room door opened and Olivia Langdon appeared, talking as she entered.

"Charles, did I hear you speaking to someone?"

He stiffened. "Yes, Mother."

Olivia looked up and saw Mark—the same instant Mark turned and saw Olivia. "Oh," she said in a small, bewildered voice, "is *this* your guest?"

"Yes, Mother," Charlie answered, swallowing a lump in his throat.

Without looking around, Olivia reached behind her back and closed the dining room door.

"This is my friend Mark Twain," Charlie continued miserably. "I was just taking him up to his room to—uh—wash up a little."

Mark removed the hat and bowed. "Good evening, Mrs. Langdon. I'm delighted to meet you at last."

Olivia managed a chilly smile. "How do you do, Mr. Clemens? I hope you will find your room comfortable."

"Thank you. I don't imagine you'll hear any serious complaints."

"Mark'll be down in a few minutes, Mother," Charlie said, adding meaningfully to Mark, "You won't be long, *will* you?"

"No, Charlie, I'll be more or less respectable in no time." Mark leaned around Charlie. "You won't recognize me next time you see me, Mrs. Langdon. Charlie will probably have to introduce us all over again." He turned and started up the stairs. "All right, Charlie, lead me to the soap and water."

With a helpless glance at his mother, Charlie tagged along behind Mark. Olivia watched them until they disappeared down the hall. Then, after standing uncertainly for a moment, she opened the dining room door and rejoined Livy and Jervis.

"Ah, my dear," said Jervis, "have you had enough of *Bleak House* for the evening?"

"Yes, thank you." She lowered her voice. "Jervis, Mr. Clemens has arrived."

He closed the volume. "He has? Splendid."

"Where is he, Mother?" Livy asked eagerly.

"Charles took him up to his room."

"Did you meet him?"

"Yes—fleetingly."

"Did you like him?"

Her mother hesitated. "Well, he seemed—courteous. I really didn't have time to form an opinion."

"You'll find him refreshing, I think," Langdon said. "He has an oblique, earthy kind of wit that's most unusual. At least in this part of the country."

Olivia nodded. "I did have time to notice that."

Livy was smiling. "Charlie says he's the most amusing conversationalist he's ever met."

Her mother gave her a sidelong glance. "And what about Mr. Clemens's *letters,* my dear? Are they amusing as well?"

Livy considered her answer carefully. "They're amusing only occasionally, Mother. Mostly they're serious and thoughtful. But," she added hastily, "all of them are beautifully written."

Hearing Charlie coming down the stairs, they moved back into the drawing room.

"Mark says he'll be down in a few minutes," Charlie announced. "And he gave me a message for you." He imitated Mark's drawl: "He said, 'Charlie, tell your folks not to say anything disputatious till I get there, because I always hate to miss a good family argument.' "

Livy and her father laughed heartily. "By George," Jervis said, "that's exactly what Mr. Clemens *would* say."

"But what did he mean?" Olivia asked perplexedly. "I don't believe we've *ever* argued."

"He was only joking, Mother," Charlie explained. "Don't you see? It's what they call a typical Twainian remark."

"Oh yes, I see," she said without conviction.

"How does Mark look?" Livy wanted to know. "I haven't seen him since New Year's Day."

"He looks just great," Charlie answered, "doesn't he, Mother?"

"Yes, Charles, he seemed to be in good health, but" —she hesitated, frowning—"what was that peculiar yellowish garment he was wearing?"

"Oh, he calls that his travel shroud."

Jervis exploded a laugh and slapped his knee. "Travel shroud! Ha—that's rich—really rich!"

"It's actually a duster," Charlie said. "He wears it to cover his clothes when he rides on trains."

His mother smiled faintly. "What he really needs is something to cover the duster."

While waiting for Mark to join them, the Langdons discussed plans for his entertainment. At length he appeared at the top of the stairs looking well scrubbed and wearing a dark suit, white shirt, and black string tie.

"Come on down, Mark," Charlie called, immensely relieved by his guest's transformation.

"Hallelujah!" Mark exclaimed. "At last I'm privileged to see the whole Langdon family together."

"And not arguing, either," Charlie pointed out.

"Well, don't hold back on my account. The wrangle can start any time you're ready."

Livy neatened her hair and smoothed her skirt as Mark came down the stairs. Jervis stepped forward and gave him a warm handshake. "Mr. Clemens, I'm happy to see you again."

"Thank you, sir, I'm right happy myself." To Olivia he said quizzically, "Recognize me now, Mrs. Langdon?"

"Perfectly, Mr. Clemens. Welcome to our home." Mark took her outstretched hand and bowed. "Thank you, I was a long time getting here." He saved his greeting for Livy until last, and as he turned to her, his face softened. "And how is my lovely and faithful correspondent?"

"I'm well thank you, Mark." She flushed slightly as he took her hand and held it. "We're so pleased to have you here at last."

"I've been looking forward to it for a long time, Livy," he said fervently.

She cast a shy glance at her parents and drew her hand back.

"I thought you'd never come to Elmira, Mark," Charlie said. "It took you seven months to accept my last invitation."

Mark shrugged. "Well, Charlie, time is relative—to use an expression invented by the railroads. Just my trip today from New York seemed like seven months." He turned to Olivia. "I know I was expected in time for dinner, Mrs. Langdon. The trouble was the New York Central didn't know it."

She clucked her tongue. "That awful railroad—really. Why don't you speak to them, Jervis?"

"I fully intend to, my dear. Their service is becoming abominable."

"Their locomotives are the weariest in the country,"

Mark said. "I was on one of those trains that gets tired every seven minutes and stops to rest three-quarters of an hour."

Jervis chuckled. "That's typical. I know exactly what you mean."

"I just hope it wasn't your coal they were using, Mr. Langdon."

"My coal?" He grinned. "Oh, I see what you mean. No, the New York Central doesn't use my coal, but I wish it did—I'd retire."

"Oh dear," Livy said suddenly, "it just occurred to me, Mark—after that long trip you must be hungry as a bear. Cook's gone to bed, but I could manage something for you to eat."

Mark shook his head. "That's kind of you, Livy, but I couldn't swallow another thing." He rubbed his stomach cautiously. "I had a couple of those concrete sandwiches on the train."

Livy indicated a chair. "In that case, you poor man, you'd better sit down and recover."

"Let's all make ourselves comfortable," her mother said.

As they seated themselves, Mark disregarded the chair and settled down beside Livy on the divan. "Ah, this is pure luxury. If the railroads had seats like these, I wouldn't mind traveling."

"I should think you'd get used to traveling," Charlie said. "I hear you've done plenty of it since I saw you last."

"That's right, I've been out to San Francisco and all

points in between. I never get a chance to light in one place for any decent length of time."

"My daughter tells me," said Mrs. Langdon, "you've been making frequent appearances on lecture platforms."

"That's true. I've been airing my arrogance in public three times a week. Some nights I get out of town just ahead of the local police."

Livy made an impatient sound. "Oh, Mark, there you go belittling yourself again." She explained to her parents: "He's always doing that in his letters, and I'm always urging him to have more confidence in himself."

"I try, Livy," Mark said with a straight face, "I try every morning. I always get out of bed confident—but then I look in the mirror and get whittled right down again."

Jervis was convinced that Mark was speaking seriously. "I can't understand your self-effacing attitude, Mr. Clemens. After all, you're a man of considerable fame and literary accomplishment."

Mark grunted. "Thank you, sir, but my only literary accomplishment, if you can call it such, is one spindly book about a bullfrog lined with buckshot."

"But that isn't true," Livy argued. "Your travel letters from the *Quaker City* have been highly praised all over the country."

"But not by the *Quaker City* passengers. Most of them wish I'd fallen overboard in shark-infested waters."

Charlie laughed. "Say, Mark, do you ever see any of our happy pilgrims from the boat?"

"I come across Dan Slote fairly often when I'm in New York. And Jack Van Nostrand came to see me when I lectured near his home town." Absently, Mark drew a cigar from his inner pocket and rolled it between his fingers. "They both asked about you, Charlie —wondered if I'd seen you." He turned to Livy. "They inquired about you, too. They spoke of you as 'the raving beauty of the portrait.' I told them I agreed with that description of you and—" He stopped, aware that Livy was wrinkling her nose at the cigar and that her parents had assumed expressions of disapproval. "And," he continued smoothly, "that you'd written me suggesting that I quit smoking." Returning the cigar to his pocket, he addressed Olivia. "You should be proud of your daughter, Mrs. Langdon. She's a talented reformer."

Olivia inclined her head slightly. "Her father and I have always done our best to bring her up sensibly, Mr. Clemens."

Realizing that he had stepped back from the brink of a disastrous faux pas, Mark wiped his forehead and switched the subject. "Livy, you just spoke favorably of those travel letters of mine. It might interest you to know that I've turned them into a book and never wrote you a single word about it. It's a surprise."

"Mark—that's a splendid idea."

"A whole book about our trip?" Charlie asked excitedly. "We'll buy at least ten copies, won't we, Father?"

"A dozen, if they're inscribed by the author."

"Sounds like a pretty good proposition, Mr. Langdon," Mark said. "You keep buying and I'll keep inscribing till the inkwell runs dry."

Jervis smiled. "I think a dozen will satisfy us. Have you found a publisher?"

"Yes, sir, I hooked a pretty good one at a time when his resistance was low. Elisha Bliss, over in Hartford."

"Oh yes, I know Bliss—a shrewd, capable man. American Publishing Company—reliable firm. I hope you managed a favorable contract."

"We were both satisfied, I think. At least no blood was shed at the signing."

"As a businessman," Jervis continued, "I'm interested in how book publishers arrange payments these days. Don't mean to pry, of course."

"Pry right ahead. I think that if you want to know something, there's no harm in asking right out. Bliss gave me my choice of two propositions: ten thousand dollars cash for my copyright or a five percent royalty. I must confess I was dazzled by the idea of the cash . . ."

Langdon cut in, "But you chose the royalty scheme, I hope?"

"Yes, sir, I did, and I just hope I won't live to regret it."

"Good reasoning, Mr. Clemens. You won't regret it, I assure you—not with that excellent source material."

"Am I in the book?" Charlie asked eagerly.

"I daren't keep you out, Charlie, if you buy all those copies. But you're in it for sure—you, Dan, Jack, the doctor—all the decent people."

Livy touched Mark's arm. "I'm really delighted about the book, Mark. I'm sure it will be an enormous success."

"Thanks, Livy, but I'm not counting my chickens. Word has leaked out in certain quarters that my material is too irreverent to be popular. Even my title has raised a few pious eyebrows." He took a deep breath. "I'm calling it *The New Pilgrim's Progress.*"

"Oh dear," Olivia said, "that *is* irreverent."

"Why do you say that, Mother?" Charlie demanded. "I think it's a great title. Don't you, Father?"

Jervis tugged thoughtfully at his beard. "I'm not sure, Charlie—your mother may be right." He turned to Mark. "Who are the people that are objecting to the material?"

"According to Bliss the whole publishing fraternity. They've heard reports about the book, and some of them even say it's blasphemous in tone. Even the directors of Bliss's company are against publishing it."

"But what's Bliss's stand? After all, he's the man who liked it from the beginning."

"Bliss is on my side, of course. He believes so strongly in the book that he said if his company won't publish it, he'll resign and publish it himself. But I think it's my title that bothers people most. Livy, what's your opinion? Does the title offend you?"

81

Livy wrinkled her forehead. "That's really beside the point, Mark—I'm thinking of the public. If a less irreverent title would sell more books, then I suggest you find one."

Mark threw his head back and guffawed. "Well, I'll be jiggered. I never dreamt that behind that comely brow there lies a mind that's concerned with profit and loss."

"She's her father's daughter, Mr. Clemens," Jervis said proudly.

"All right, Livy," Mark continued, "if your commercial instinct suggests that my title be changed, I'd be a fool to disregard it. Another title popped into my head while I was on the train, and I wrote it down." He took a small slip of paper from his pocket and handed it to her. "Here—how's this for a substitute?"

She considered the title for a moment, then read it aloud: *"The Innocents Abroad."* Handing the slip back, she said decisively, "That's it, Mark."

Her mother was pleased. "Oh, that's a much nicer title, isn't it, Jervis?"

Langdon tried it on his tongue: *"The Innocents Abroad.* . . . Hm . . . yes, that's excellent."

"I still like the first one best," Charlie muttered.

"Too late, Charlie," Mark said with a grin. "Livy's my counselor now." Charlie scowled and slouched to the window, where he stood peering out into the darkness. Mark dug into his pocket and brought out several pages of manuscript. "For my final draft of the book,

I'll need a number of new connecting chapters. I managed to scribble this one on the train." He handed the pages to Livy. "Here, Miss Editor, would you care to look it over?"

"I'd love to, Mark, if my parents will forgive me for a moment."

Her father was pleased by her practical interest in the book. "Of course, Livy, go right ahead; take all the time you need. Your mother and I understand, don't we, dear?"

"Why yes, Jervis," Olivia replied, not quite understanding but feeling that perhaps her husband was right as usual. "Livy, dear, while you're reading Mr. Clemens's—uh—story, I'll go and put an extra leaf in the dining room table for morning. I noticed that Nora's forgotten it, even after I gave her careful instructions."

Jervis gestured to capture Charlie's attention and pointed toward the dining room. "Charlie, you might go and help your mother."

"Yes, sir," Charlie replied, almost sullenly. Following his mother to the door, he called pointedly over his shoulder, "I'll be right back, Mark."

Mark gave a careless wave of dismissal. "Take your time, Charlie—there's no hurry."

Charlie cast a troubled glance at his father and went into the dining room. Jervis opened a book and began to read, while Livy and Mark settled back on the divan and conversed in low tones.

"I'm eager to read what you've written, Mark," Livy told him. "It's all very exciting."

He stared at her, shaking his head in disbelief. "Livy, how beautiful you look! Even lovelier than I remembered."

The suddenness of his remark disturbed her. "Why —thank you." She glanced across at her father and opened the manuscript. "Shall I read this aloud or to myself?"

"Whatever you like, Livy. But wait—before you begin." He took the manuscript and placed it beside him. Reaching into his waistcoat pocket, he brought out a small plush box and handed it to her. "I brought this for you. Bless you, dear sister."

"Mark—what is it?"

"Open it and see."

Livy pushed back the lid, gave a gasp, and took out a bracelet with a tiny gold pendant. "Why, Mark—it's lovely."

His attention arrested by the excitement in her voice, her father looked up, then looked down again at the book.

"Hold out your arm," Mark said gently, and as she did so, he fastened the bracelet around her wrist. "I had it made for you." He nudged the pendant with a finger. "This little do-jigger that hangs down is gold I took out of the earth."

"Really?"

"Really and truly," he said, adding apologetically, "It

isn't big enough to fill a back tooth, but it's the only paydirt I ever dug up in California."

Livy studied the bracelet admiringly. "Thank you, Mark, I love it. But I never expected you to bring me a gift."

"It's not a gift, it's a reward."

She frowned. "A reward? What for?"

"For reading and answering all those dry letters of mine. You were a diligent and welcome correspondent during those lonely months."

"Your letters weren't dry, Mark—they were fascinating."

He gave her a guilty glance. "I admit, though, I had a hard time keeping them 'just friendly,' as I'd promised to do."

"Yes," Livy said shyly, "I noticed that."

"But each time I began a letter with 'my dear sister,' my heart took over my pen. Were you offended?"

"No," Livy confessed, "merely confused."

Her father was trying decently not to eavesdrop, yet he was tremendously interested in the bits of conversation he had been unable to screen out. Shifting into another position, he attempted to concentrate fully upon his book, but being unable to do so, he was relieved when Olivia and Charlie returned from their chore in the dining room.

The men rose to their feet, and Livy sprang up with her arm outstretched. "Look, everybody—Mark brought me the dearest present."

"A bracelet," Olivia said in surprise. "Well, well."

"A present?" Charlie said. "What for?"

"Well, Charlie," Mark explained, "let's say it's for your sister's birthday, whenever that comes."

Jervis took Livy's wrist and scrutinized the bracelet carefully. "What's this?" he asked, pointing to the pendant. "It looks like a gold nugget."

"It is a gold nugget," Mark said. "I dug it up at a place called Jackass Hill." He smiled at Livy. "But I won't belittle myself about that—it was named Jackass Hill long before I got there."

Jervis chortled. "Long before you got there. Ha-ha—that's very good—really rich."

Olivia smiled politely, and Charlie merely scowled.

"Goodness," Livy said, picking up Mark's manuscript, "in all the excitement I still haven't read your new chapter. I was going to read it aloud, but"—she glanced at her mother—"first perhaps I'd better read it to myself."

"Oh, my," Mark said apprehensively, "I fear the worst. I see a censorial glint in your eye."

"Editorial," Livy corrected him smilingly, "not censorial." She looked about uncertainly, then spoke to Jervis. "Do you mind if we use your study for a little while?"

Charlie glared at his father, awaiting his answer. "Why, no, I suppose not," Jervis said finally. "Help yourselves."

"Thank you," Livy said. "Will you excuse us, Mother? We won't be long. Come on, Mark."

Mark bowed to Olivia and followed Livy into the study, closing the door. Olivia gave her husband a reproachful look and waited suspensefully to hear what he might have to say.

Jervis took a turn about the room, fingering his beard fiercely. "Charlie," he said in guarded tones, "for what length of time did you ask Mr. Clemens to stay here as your guest?"

"Until tomorrow night," Charlie answered darkly. "Why?"

His father sighed. "Because it appears to me that he's campaigning to capture our Livy."

"Me too!" Charlie snapped.

His mother grasped the back of a chair. "Jervis! Are you sure?"

"Ninety-nine percent."

"But," she protested, "the poor child isn't strong enough to marry *anyone*. Particularly that—" She broke off, motioning feebly toward the study door.

"It's all my fault," Charlie moaned. "I invited him. What're we going to do?"

Jervis hunched his shoulders. "She's twenty-two, Charlie, and she has a mind of her own."

"I know, but—" He turned away, pounding the arm of a chair.

Olivia walked unsteadily to the staircase. "Jervis, I'm afraid I don't feel very well. Will you make my excuses, please?"

"You stay and see to it, Charlie," his father directed. "I'll look after your mother."

"Yes, *sir*," Charlie assured him grimly. "I'll stay right here till they come out."

Supporting Olivia with one arm, Jervis helped her up the steps. Charlie watched them until they turned the corner of the upstairs hall, then sat down heavily in the chair nearest the door of the study.

Despite his admiration for Mark Twain, Charlie was truly alarmed. During the *Quaker City* voyage the two had shared the fun and the misery for almost six months, and Mark had been not only Charlie's companion but his hero as well. Livy, however, was a saint in Charlie's eyes, and no man, not even a true hero, was good enough to be her husband. He had boasted all over Elmira that the famous Mark Twain, his personal friend, was coming to town as his guest; but now that he was here, Charlie wished he had never come and cursed himself for having endangered his sister's purity. Mark Twain was undoubtedly a great man, but no fit life companion for the sainted Livy. Such was Charlie's dilemma as he stood guard outside the study door, repeatedly jamming a fist into his hand.

7

EARLY the next morning in his room above the carriage house, the Langdons' coachman smelled cigar smoke drifting up from the ground floor. Going to the stairwell, he called down, "Mornin', Mr. Twain."

"Good morning, Barney," Mark replied as the delighted Irishman came hurrying down. "How'd you know it was me?"

"Ha—'cause it couldn't've been Mr. L. smoking that cigar, God knows—nor Charlie, nor for that matter any other member of the Park Congregationalist Church, the Reverend Thomas K. Beecher, pastor."

"Sorry to defile your premises," Mark said, exhaling a blue cloud, "but until I get a cigar stoked up in the morning, my brain refuses to set foot out of bed. Have one for yourself?"

"No thanks, Mr. Twain. It ain't that I wouldn't like to, but if either the Mister or the Missus ever caught me smokin' on this property, they'd skin me alive."

"I've heard that's fairly painful," Mark observed. "But tell me, are you allowed to smoke at your local barbershop?"

"Oh, sure. They're all nice intelligent boys down there, thank God."

"Then take this cigar, and if you have time, drive me to the barbershop and we'll smoke together."

"Thanks, Mr. Twain, I'll do that and enjoy it. I'm on my own time this mornin'. Mr. L. walks to his office, and Mrs. L. never needs me till afternoon." Barney was gleeful as he harnessed the horse. "The boys down at the barbershop are in for a rare surprise, and that's the truth. I told 'em Mark Twain was here, visitin' young Charlie, and they was wishin' they could see you. So when you walk in as big as life, you can bet they'll be tickled silly."

"That'll be fine, Barney, but let's hope the barber won't be too tickled to shampoo the coal dust out of this mop of mine."

When they were ready to climb into the carriage, Barney jerked a thumb at Mark's cigar. "I don't mean to be bossy, Mr. Twain, but before we go past the house, you better duck that stogie."

Mark ground the half-smoked cigar under his shoe. "Thanks for the warning. I'm not very partial to being skinned alive myself."

While they were driving downtown, Barney identified Elmira's chief points of interest. "That red buildin' there, that's the public liberry; and the wooden one across from it, that's our high school. On your left, down here in the next block—that's the Elmira National Bank." He added proudly, "I happen to be acquainted in a small way with the president of that bank. Name's Mr. Barton. A couple times a year he comes to the Langdons' for Sunday dinner."

"Very interesting," Mark said, "but have you ever tried to borrow money from him?"

"Me? From Mr. Barton? God save me, I should say not." He grinned. "Even if I had nerve enough, I wouldn't dare. Just between me and you, he's kind of a skinflint."

Mark nodded knowingly. "He's got skinflint-itis—an occupational disease that afflicts almost all bankers. You know, Barney, I once knew a banker who was proud of a glass eye that had been made for him by the greatest artist in Paris, France. When I asked him to lend me some money, he said, 'Son, I'll give it to you if you can guess which of my eyes is the glass one.' I said, 'It's the left eye, of course. It's the only one with a glint of human kindness in it.'"

As Barney had predicted, the boys at the barbershop were elated when the famous visitor walked in. The news spread quickly around the neighborhood, and soon after the shampoo got under way, the small shop was crowded with raucous but respectful admirers. Some shouted, "What happened to the jumpin' frog?" while others cried, "Did you bring that old bullfrog with you, Mark?" . . . "Hey, Mark, are your pants pockets loaded with buckshot?"

In the company of men who exactly suited him, Mark joked and smoked with them for a long time.

Noting that several of the younger ones were wearing odd remnants of their Union Army uniforms, he was "reminded" of his own brief service on the side of the Rebels during the War Between the States.

"There was a time," he began, "when the very sight of a Union cap like the one this young fellow is wearing would've scared the gizzard out of me. That was in the spring of '61, when my home state of Missouri was invaded by the Union forces. The governor sent out a call for volunteers to help repel the invader, so I came back to Hannibal, in Marion County, and joined up with a bunch of about fifteen local boys. We met one dark night in the woods and formed a military company which we called the Marion Rangers."

After Mark's listeners had finished taunting him for having been a "Johnny Reb," he again took up his narrative. The Marion Rangers, he explained, thought the war was going to be a kind of picnic. They had no idea who the invader was that they were supposed to repel, except that it was a bunch of nasty characters called "Feds." While they were appointing officers—no member of the unit would consent to be a private—young Sam Clemens announced that he was a born second lieutenant, and got the job. When he learned that there were five Feds in the vicinity, just itching to shoot some Rebs, Sam suggested a shrewd military maneuver: retreat.

Several days later, encamped in a miserable spot that Sam called Camp Devastation, they heard that a Union general was galloping in their direction "with a whole big goddam regiment." Thinking clearly once again, Sam advised that they execute the classical military maneuver for the second time, and off the fifteen warriors went, in fifteen different directions.

At this point in Mark's narrative the barbershop boys were roaring with laughter. "I never did like the idea of killing strangers anyway," he concluded, "so that was the end of the Marion Rangers. I could've been a soldier if I'd waited around—I'd got part of it learned: I knew more about retreating than the man that invented retreating."

After buying and distributing a box of cigars, Mark said good-bye and was escorted out to the carriage by the cheering boys of the barbershop.

"By granny," he told Barney as the horse trotted up the street toward the Langdon house, "I haven't had such a good time since my congressman's funeral."

When he learned from Livy that her mother was not feeling well and would spend the day in bed, Mark was properly sympathetic, but recovered his high spirits when Livy suggested that they stroll around the grounds before luncheon and tell each other about their lives before they met. Mark approved of her plan and accepted it without revisions.

Charlie joined them at the luncheon table but ate quickly, said very little, and excused himself as soon as he had bolted his peach cobbler.

After the meal Livy gathered writing materials and

told Mark she would like to work with him on the manuscript, in accordance with the notes she had written in the margins the night before. The thought of being alone with her again delighted him, and when she suggested that the ideal spot for uninterrupted concentration would be the summer house, he agreed that it was a splendid idea.

Seated side by side at a rustic table, they took turns reading aloud. Whenever they arrived at a word, phrase, or sentence that struck Livy as coarse or tasteless—and there were many indelicacies in Mark's early work—she would halt the reading and supervise the reconstruction until she was satisfied with its literary purity. If, after a certain amount of creative labor, no improvement was noted, Livy simply took her pen and struck out the offending phrase.

Following one excision Mark raised his voice in mock protest. "Livy! What're you doing to me? Don't you realize it took me five minutes to word that tiny phrase?"

"What does it matter?" she asked calmly. "Would you rather lose five minutes or five hundred readers?"

He laughed and handed her the pen. "Here—cut two more phrases and gain me a thousand readers. Or better yet—tear up the whole manuscript and gain me the entire population of New York State."

So smooth was their collaboration as author and editor that the afternoon flew by without their being aware of its passing. The result of their labor was a chapter that set a worthy pattern for Mark to follow throughout the writing of the final draft of the book.

At the dinner table that evening, Mark praised Livy's editorial acumen to her father and brother. Charlie listened politely without comment, but Jervis Langdon was delighted with this additional proof of his daughter's critical perception.

"How unfortunate that your mother could not be with us, Livy," he said. "She would be as proud of you as I am. What about you, Charlie? Aren't you pleased to learn about your sister's talent?"

"Yes, Father," Charlie replied, without glancing up from his chop, "I think it's great."

After dinner, shortly before Barney was to drive Mark to the railroad station to catch the New York sleeper, Mark went upstairs to pack his valise. When Barney came in from the driveway, he glanced around the empty drawing room, then went to the study and knocked.

"Yes?" came Jervis's voice.

"Barney out here, Mr. Langdon. Sorry to bother you."

Jervis emerged. "Ready to leave?"

"Yes, sir, I hitched up the two-seater. I figgered that'd be just the ticket, seein' as Mr. Twain's only got the one valise. He can sit in the back seat, and the valise can ride up front with me."

"Very well, Barney." Langdon looked at his watch. "Mr. Twain should be ready to leave in a very few minutes now."

"Yes, sir, I'll be waitin' right outside." He took a step

toward the door and turned back. "Oh, I meant to ask, Mr. Langdon—how's the Missus feelin' tonight?"

"Fairly well, thank you, Barney."

"Nothin' serious, I hope?"

"No, just a minor nervous upset."

"That's good, thank God. Will she be able to get around soon?"

"Yes, I'm quite sure she will. The doctor promised she'll be up and active in a day or two."

Barney grinned. "It's too bad Mr. Twain ain't her doctor."

"Mr. Twain? I don't understand."

"Well, you know, sir—they say laughter's the best medicine."

"So I've heard. But in Mrs. Langdon's case I think I'll put my trust in Dr. Harris."

"Yes, sir, I see what you mean. But that Mark Twain is a lalapalooza. I sure never thought I'd get a chance to meet a famous feller like him, and yet here he is, right here in Elmira and under our roof."

"He's a brilliant man, Barney—there's no denying that."

"You know, sir, I was thinkin'—it's a big feather in Charlie's cap to have such a man for a friend. Ain't he excited?"

"Excited?" Jervis chose his words carefully. "Well, let's say he's greatly—uh—stimulated by Mr. Clemens's visit."

Barney was eager to boast about his own friendship

with Elmira's celebrity. "Mr. Twain come out to the carriage house this mornin' to see me, would you believe it?"

"Yes, Barney, I think I would."

"He asked me to drive him down to the barbershop if I had time to spare. I said I did, so I drove him. And all the way down he kept me laughin' with his jokes."

Mr. Langdon smiled. "I know what you mean—he has a full stock of them, one for every occasion I should think."

"You're right, sir. When we drove by the Elmira National, he had one about a banker that was a humdinger."

Langdon's eyes twinkled. "Oh yes, about an umbrella?"

"No, sir, about a glass eye."

Langdon seemed disappointed. "Oh—he didn't tell me that one."

"Anyway, sir," Barney continued, "when he walked into the barbershop, every last one of the boys recognized him as Mark Twain"—he snapped his fingers—"just like that. And the whole entire time he was in the chair he kept everybody roarin'. I sure wish he was goin' to stay in Elmira, Mr. Langdon—I bet the whole town'd come to life. It's a real shame he's leavin'."

"Yes it is, Barney, but I have a feeling he'll be back before long."

"I sure hope so, sir." As Barney turned to leave,

Charlie came down the stairs. "Oh, I got the wagon outside, Charlie. Is Mr. T. almost ready?"

"Yes, he'll be down in a minute."

Barney pointed to Charlie in surprise. "Hey, you shaved off your moustache. What for?"

"I got tired of it," Charlie answered sharply.

"Oh." Perplexed by the boy's curt manner, Barney glanced at Mr. Langdon, who looked away. "Anyway, Charlie, call me when Mr. Twain's ready." With another glance at Mr. Langdon, Barney went out, shaking his head.

"Where's Livy?" Charlie asked.

"She took a cup of hot broth up to your mother."

"Well, she'd better come down soon. Mark will raise Cain if *she* isn't here to say good-bye."

His father spoke brusquely. "Charlie, while we're waiting, I'd like to speak to you about Mr. Clemens."

Charlie stared at the wall. "What about him?"

"I want you to bear in mind that he is our guest and, as such, deserves courteous treatment."

"What do you mean?" Charlie asked peevishly. "I've been polite to him, haven't I?"

"A bit too polite, in fact. I'm sure he's noticed the abrupt change in your attitude."

"What about his attitude toward me? He doesn't give a hang about me."

"Nonsense, Charlie. He's extremely fond of you, or he wouldn't have come here in the first place."

Charlie grunted. "You don't think he came here to see *me*, do you?"

"I think he came to see both you and your sister."

"Oh, sure—and he sat in the summer house with Livy all afternoon. Every time I walked by they were working on his damn book."

Jervis bridled. "Son, I've told you never to use that word."

"Why not?" Charlie asked belligerently. "*He* uses it all the time."

"But obviously he's no longer your model." He indicated Charlie's bare upper lip. "Even Barney noticed the loss of your moustache."

Charlie's finger went to his lip. "You don't think I shaved this off because—"

He stopped as Mark came down the staircase with his valise. The duster and straw hat were rolled up under one arm. "Well, Langdons, father and son," Mark said, "I'm about to check out of your high-class hotel. I must say I'm greatly pleased with it, the low room rates in particular. But, Charlie, before I go, hadn't you better run up and count the towels?"

Charlie glared. "We're not worried about our towels —*they're* not family treasures."

"Charlie!" his father murmured in soft admonishment.

Mark shot an amused glance at Charlie and spoke sincerely to Jervis. "I'm sorry about Mrs. Langdon's indisposition. Won't you thank her for her hospitality and tell her I wish her a rapid recovery?"

"I will, Mr. Clemens. She'll be most grateful for your thoughtfulness."

The men turned as Livy came down, carrying her mother's tray. "Well, Mark," she said regretfully, "I see you're ready to leave us."

"Yes, Livy, I'm all packed up and dreading another skirmish with the railroad. I'd like to give you a farewell handshake, if you can manage it."

"Of course. Just let me put this tray down."

"Charlie," Jervis said, "wouldn't you like to take that tray out to the kitchen for your sister?" Charlie scowled and complied reluctantly. "I'd better give the boy some assistance," Jervis added, with a knowing smile at Mark. "I doubt he's any too familiar with the kitchen."

"Livy," Mark said, "there goes a man of magnificent perception. For giving us a private moment he deserves a good mark from St. Peter—or whoever it is that keeps the records up yonder." He took Livy's hands. "Well, dear sister, I've always dreaded good-byes. And this one is more distressing to me than any other."

She looked up at him. "You won't stop writing me, will you, Mark?"

"Not so long as I'm able to hold a pen."

"Will you send me the proofs of your book when you get them, and your new additions as soon as you've written them?"

"I'll mail you *something* every day, Livy—if only for the joy of writing your name on the envelope."

"I'm terribly anxious to see the manuscript you gave the publisher."

"And I want you to see it because I'm sure it needs lots of your style of laundering. When you get the printed proofs, you'll notice they have wide margins for that very purpose."

"Mark—promise me you won't be angry if I mail them back to you with my 'editorial suggestions'?"

"Angry? Dear girl, I'll accept every suggestion you make without the usual author's argument." Mark bent close and spoke earnestly. "But I'll want something more from you in your letters, Livy—something of yourself."

She drew back a little. "But I'm afraid I won't have anything to say about myself."

He raised his voice. "Then write me passages from the Good Book—or even sermons on the evils of drink —it won't matter as long as the words are set down by your hand. Will you do that, Livy—will you?"

"Yes, Mark," she said softly, "I'll try."

Mark had just completed writing his list of mailing addresses for Livy when her father returned, followed by Charlie. "Well, Mr. Clemens," Langdon said, "you'd better get started."

"Yes, sir, the railroad waits for neither man nor beast."

Charlie opened the front door impatiently and started out. "I'll tell Barney you're coming." His voice was heard from the driveway. "All right, Barney, he's ready to go."

Mark shook Langdon's hand. "Good-bye to you, sir —warm thanks to you."

"It was my pleasure, Mr. Clemens—uh—mine and Mrs. Langdon's. Safe journey."

"Thank you." Mark spoke to Livy in a low voice. "Stay well, won't you?"

"Wait," she said, "I'm coming out with you. I'll be right back, Father."

Mark lifted his valise, exchanged a parting nod with Jervis, and followed Livy through the door. Behind them Jervis called out, "Barney."

"Yes, sir?"

"Pick up a newspaper at the depot, will you?"

"Sure thing, Mr. Langdon." The skittish horse jerked the wagon forward as Mark climbed aboard. "Easy, girl, easy there."

The mare continued her nervous capering as Mark settled in the back seat. "Easy, Bessie!" Barney growled. "Ready, Mr. Twain?"

"Yes, Barney, let 'er rip."

Mark let go of the seat to wave good-bye, and as he did so, Barney slapped the reins. With a frightened neigh, the mare sprang forward.

"Look out!" Charlie yelled.

"Whoa!" Barney shouted. "Whoa!"

But it was too late. Both Mark and the seat described a backward arc and landed heavily on the stony drive.

Livy screamed shrilly, *"Mark!"*

"Gosh almighty!" Charlie exclaimed.

"Holy Mother of God!" Barney said in a strangled voice. Leaping to the ground, he tied the mare to the hitching post and ran back to assess the damage.

"He's unconscious," Charlie said. "He landed on the back of his head."

"Father!" Livy screamed. "Help!"

Langdon's horrified voice came from the darkness at the top of the steps. "Livy! Are you hurt?"

"No, it's Mark."

"He fell backward off the wagon," Charlie cried.

"*What?*"

"On his head," Barney added gravely.

Langdon hurried down the steps, almost colliding with Livy on her way into the house. "Livy—how did it happen?"

"The horse bolted." Suddenly in control of herself, Livy took charge and issued crisp orders. "Bring him inside, Father—you and Charlie and Barney. Carry him carefully now—mind what I say. I'll arrange a place in the drawing room." Rushing across to the divan, she fluffed a cushion for Mark's head, then raced back to the kitchen.

In the murky driveway the three men bent over the inert figure. "Now we'll lift him," Jervis said. "But gently—very gently. I'll take his head. Ready?"

"Yes, sir," Barney said. "I got his feet."

"Charlie," his father directed, "you do what you can with the middle."

Charlie leaned down. "All right, Father, I've got it— let's go."

With a great deal of straining and grunting, the men lifted Mark and carried him up the steps. "Careful now," Langdon warned. "Let's be sure to clear the doorframe."

"I don't know how it happened," Barney muttered.

"All of a sudden Bessie jumped, and the next thing I knew the whole back seat shot out and the poor dear man was layin' there in a heap."

"I told you that bolt was rusted through," Jervis said accusingly.

"Yes, sir, you did, and I'll take the blame, God help me. But poor Mr. Twain—to think such a thing should happen to a man like him. If his head's cracked open, I'll never forgive myself."

Livy hurried from the kitchen with a cold towel and motioned the group to the divan. "Right down here please—very carefully—his head at this end." She arranged the pillow under Mark's head as the men lowered him slowly and stepped back looking harried and helpless. Livy knelt beside Mark and ran her fingers experimentally across his head.

Barney spoke fearfully. "Is he bleedin' much?"

"Yes, there seems to be a nasty gash."

He leaned forward in a listening attitude. "He's breathin', glory be to God."

"Barney," Langdon snapped, "don't just stand there muttering. Go fetch Dr. Harris."

"Yes, sir, I'll do that, sir." He raced out the door. "I'll run all the way, God help me."

Livy applied the towel to Mark's head and glanced up at Charlie. "Get me another damp towel."

"Sure." He was ashen and his voice trembled. "You want cold water?"

"Don't argue, Charlie!" his father said. "Just go and get it."

"Yes, sir." He scurried out to the kitchen.

"Father," Livy said, "I'm sure that when Dr. Harris comes, he'll want to put Mark to bed. Would you go up please and make sure his room is in order?"

"Of course, my dear, at once." He was ascending the staircase when Olivia appeared in a negligee on the top landing. "Olivia," he said, startled, "you were not supposed to get out of bed."

"I heard shouting in the driveway, Jervis. What happened?"

"Don't talk now, my dear—just let me help you back to your room." Taking the bewildered woman by the arm, he was about to lead her away when she glanced down and saw Livy kneeling beside the recumbent Mark, stroking his forehead.

"Jervis!" she cried, pointing, dumbfounded. *"Look!"*

"I know," he said, urging her forward. "I know all about it."

Olivia whimpered. "But—what are Livy and Mr. Clemens *doing?*"

"It's a long, complicated story, my love," he answered, leading her along the hallway. "I'll explain it all to you when you're back in bed."

In the drawing room Mark groaned and his eyelids fluttered. "Lie still," Livy said softly. "You're going to be all right."

He opened his eyes and frowned, unable to focus clearly. "Is it—Livy?"

"Yes, Mark."

"But—what happened?"

"You had a nasty fall."

His frown slowly gave way to a grin. "So did Adam —but Eve didn't give him *this* kind of attention."

Livy smiled and laid her palm gently on his lips. "Sh, Mark—just try to be still for a while."

8

THE news of Mark Twain's accident appeared on the front page of the local paper and was reprinted by major journals throughout the country. Dr. Harris, who achieved out-of-town notoriety for the first (and last) time in his career, announced that the Langdon family's prominent guest had suffered a mild concussion plus several minor scalp wounds and abrasions. Later in the week Mark himself confided to a visiting reporter that his neck had been broken in fourteen different places and that his doctor had warned him to stay out of those places if he didn't want to get hurt.

Dr. Harris's prognosis was that the patient would regain his health with reasonable speed, provided he be kept in bed for a week and not be permitted to travel for an additional week.

Jervis Langdon was rather pleased by the prospect of his guest's extended visit, for he respected Mark's talents and delighted in his humor and eccentricities. He felt, too, that Mark's ardor for Livy would be considerably restrained by the necessity for quiet recuperation.

Olivia Langdon accepted the situation stoically, resolving at the same time to do all in her power to protect her frail daughter from being captured and carried away by the Wild Humorist of the Pacific Slope.

As for Charlie, he had been so unmanned by Mark's spectacular backward dive onto his head that some of his resentful thoughts about sharing Mark's friendship had been knocked out of his own head. He still held fast, however, to the conviction that no man, not even his bosom friend of the *Quaker City,* was good enough to be Livy's lifelong companion.

As soon as Mark's head stopped aching, his unexpected detention delighted him. Not only was he compelled to stay under Livy's roof, but his meals, company, and conversation were furnished by the angel herself. On the fourth morning after the accident he shifted to a vertical position in bed and asked Livy to bring him pen and paper so that he could continue writing the connecting chapters required for the final draft of the book. All that day and the next he wrote almost continuously, employing Barney as a messenger every few hours to deliver batches of pages to Livy.

Barney was pathetically eager to serve Mark, for he realized that the accident had resulted from his own carelessness in not having had the wagon seat repaired. Although Jervis Langdon had not forgiven his coachman completely, Mark removed the awful burden from Barney's conscience with a joke and a wave of his hand. When Barney discovered that his soul was not going to roast in hell for his sin of omission, he dropped in at his church to give thanks. Leaving a generous offering in the poor box, he stopped off at the barbershop to furnish the boys with the latest report on Mark's progress.

Livy was in the summer house making notes on Mark's manuscript when Barney returned, carrying an immense horseshoe of flowers crossed by a red ribbon bearing the legend GET WELL MARK in gold letters.

"Barney!" Livy exclaimed. "Where in the world did that come from?"

"The boys down at the barbershop. They all put together." He stepped back a few feet and studied the floral piece with pride. "Elegant, ain't it?"

She hesitated. "And so thoughtful. How sweet of your friends to do this for Mr. Twain."

"It come straight from their hearts, Miss Livy, and that's the Lord's honest truth. They think he's the finest feller that ever come down the pike. And so do I —I chipped in six bits. How is he now? Is he still sitting' up in bed writin'?"

"He was an hour ago when I took him his luncheon tray."

"Ain't it great what happened to him? I don't mean it's great that he busted his head—I mean it's great that he's stayin' with us till he's all well again. Don't you think so?"

"Yes, Barney, but I'm not sure how he feels about it. He's a very busy man."

Barney looked at her almost mischievously. "And how do *you* feel about it?"

Livy looked down at her work. "I just want him to get well, that's all."

"And he will, with God's help and your own. It's hard work lookin' after a sick man, but I notice it agrees with you. I never seen you look prettier or healthier, and that's a fact."

"Thank you, Barney, it's sweet of you to say so." She picked up her pencil. "Now wouldn't you like to take those lovely flowers up to Mr. Twain?"

"Sure, right away. I brought a whole pile of letters that people sent him, too. And all these newspapers he asked for; he's always wantin' to know what's goin' on." He tapped the top newspaper. "I bet he'll be surprised when he sees this one. There's a piece here about him, right on the first page."

Livy was pleased. "About Mr. Twain?"

"Yeah, ain't that grand? It was wrote by some feller called"—he read the by-line laboriously—"James Russell Lowell."

"Mr. Lowell?" Livy said, greatly impressed. "Goodness."

Barney looked up in surprise. "You know him?"

She smiled with her eyes. "I've heard of him."

"Anyway, this Lowell says that the entire country was sorry to hear about Mark Twain's accident, and he hopes he'll be up and around real soon." He clucked his tongue. "Imagine that—the whole country's heard about it."

"Of course—he's a prominent literary figure. Be sure to point that story out to him, Barney. It will do him more good than a whole bottle of Dr. Harris's medicine."

"I bet it will at that. Well, I'll take the flowers and stuff up to him now. If you want me for anything, just holler up the stairs."

At Mark's room Barney leaned his head in through the doorway. "Afternoon, Mark."

"Oh, hello, Barney. I was just hoping somebody would come along and wreck my train of thought. I was daydreaming about cigars."

"You better be careful," Barney warned. "In this house even dreamin' about smokin' is a sin. Tell me somethin'—how's your head today? Does it hurt much?"

"Only when I think—so I hardly ever notice it."

Barney guffawed. "Now you're talkin' just like your old self, thank God."

"Bring the rest of your body inside," Mark said. "All I can see is the top part."

"Wait, I brung a surprise for you." Reaching around the doorframe into the hall, he brought in the floral horseshoe and set it down beside the bed.

"Barney," Mark drawled, after staring at it curiously for a moment, "if I'm to wear this funeral piece around my neck, I'll be the best-dressed corpse on the eastern seaboard."

Barney frowned. "It ain't a funeral piece, Mark, it's a good-luck piece. See? It says GET WELL MARK right here on this ribbon."

"Oh, yes, so it does. But shucks—Mrs. Langdon

really shouldn't have gone to all this trouble. Just a simple bunch of dandelions would've expressed the same sweet thought."

Barney shook his head vigorously. "This ain't from Mrs. Langdon, Mark. It's from me and the boys down at the barbershop."

"Yes, I suspected it was," Mark said, genuinely touched. "I really appreciate it, Barney. Thank the boys for me and tell them I'm sorry I talked so much when I was in there the other day."

"But they loved hearin' you. They're still laughin' about some of the things you said."

"Maybe so, but I apologize for doing all that foolish yammering. It just demonstrates the truth of a rule my mother tried to teach me, but I never learned: It's better to keep your mouth shut and appear stupid than to open it and remove all doubt."

Barney roared. "I'll tell that to the boys, you can bet. And now, Mark, is there any little thing I can do for you?"

Mark slapped the bedclothes. "Yes, dammit, you can make it possible for me to smoke a cigar. But to do that, you'd have to send all the Langdons on vacation, so I guess it's out of the question."

"Try not to think about smokin'," Barney advised. "Next week when the doctor lets you get up, you can sneak out to the carriage house and smoke all day long if you feel like it."

"All right, Barney. That'll be one way of getting even with that nasty-tempered horse of yours."

Barney raised his hand. "Please don't speak of that peevish animal, Mark—she almost murdered you that night." He picked up the newspapers. "That reminds me—there's a mention of you here." He pointed out the piece by James Russell Lowell, and Mark was pleased when he read it.

"Well now, that's mighty flattering, Barney. I'll clip this out and glue it in my scrapbook. Then my grandchildren will have something to start a fire with some day when they run out of kindling."

In the batch of letters was a fat envelope from Editor Bliss in Hartford. After expressing concern about Mark's health and his hopes for a quick recovery, Bliss wrote that he was enclosing a set of galley proofs of the first draft of the book. He suggested that Mark might look them over if he felt like working during his convalescence, and return them with any changes, additions, or deletions as soon as practicable.

Mark shifted his writing board to his knees. "Well, Barney, it looks as though I've got to get busy. If you'll just sit down there and admire my sweet-smelling horseshoe, I'll finish this page I'm writing and you can take it down to Miss Livy."

Livy was deliberating over one of Mark's constructions and chewing the end of her pencil when her mother came out from the main house. "I hate to interrupt your work, my dear," Olivia said, "but a few moments ago I saw Barney delivering some kind of floral arrangement to Mr. Clemens. It looked to me like—well—a horseshoe. Could that be possible?"

Livy laughed. "Yes, Mother, that's exactly what it was—a get-well offering from Barney and his cronies at the barbershop. It's shaped like a horseshoe for luck."

"Oh, is that it? I've never seen anything quite so ornate."

"I'm sure Mark was pleased to learn that he's so well thought of by his Elmira friends." Livy examined the point of her pencil. "Now if you'll excuse me, I'd better get back to work before he discharges me for loafing."

Her mother placed a hand gently upon Livy's arm. "My dear, hadn't you better rest a while? You mustn't wear yourself out, you know."

"But I enjoy doing this, Mother. And I'm not the least bit tired."

"Are you sure?"

"Of course. Besides, I have to keep up with Mark. He's been dashing off a new page every twenty minutes."

Olivia made a small, helpless gesture. "But I'm not sure you should even be reading this story, Livy. Mr. Clemens told us himself that it has been considered irreverent."

"And that's exactly why he's asked me to look it over. He wants me to strike out everything that seems the least bit distasteful. There's nothing really nasty or sacrilegious in the book, Mother, but Mark asked me to read it and use my own judgment. So that's what I'm doing, and I should think you'd be pleased."

"I am, dear, but"—Olivia sighed and sat down—

"these last few days have been so complicated and confusing."

Livy put her pencil down and took her mother's hand. "I'm sorry, Mother. I realize that Mark's being here has upset the household routine, but goodness knows the accident wasn't his fault."

"I know that, and I've given thanks to the Lord that it wasn't more serious."

"It was a terrible misfortune for Mark, of course, but looking on the bright side, I know it's giving him the rest I'm sure he needs."

"I'm not so certain he needs a rest," Olivia said. "It seems to me he has enough energy for two men."

Livy nodded. "But at least his being here has given all of us a chance to get to know him better."

Her mother smiled faintly. "A year ago I didn't want to know him at all."

"And now?"

"Well, having him in our home has been a novel experience, I must admit. There's activity every minute, it seems." Olivia thrust her chin slightly forward. "But I'll be greatly relieved when he's gone, Livy—and so will your father."

Livy wrinkled her forehead. "Father? Why do you say that? Father's fascinated by Mark."

"As a man with a brilliant mind—yes." Looking directly at Livy, she added simply, "But not as a suitor for his daughter."

Livy turned scarlet. "Oh, I see." She turned her head

away, half whispering, "Do you and Father look upon him as my suitor?"

"Yes, we do."

"Neither of you has mentioned that to me."

"But in private we've discussed it frequently, and at great length."

"But what prompted that conclusion? Has Mark told Father or you that his purpose in coming to Elmira was to court me?"

"Of course not, but his deep affection for you is obvious. You've had little or no experience with men, my dear, but surely you cannot be unaware of Mr. Clemens's affectionate feelings for you."

Livy swung back. "I'm not that inexperienced, Mother."

Olivia sat quietly for a moment, tapping the table with a fingernail. "Livy dear," she said at last, "tell me truthfully. Has Mr. Clemens asked you to be his wife?"

"No, not even in his letters."

"Do you think he intends to ask you?"

"Yes I do," Livy admitted, "some day."

"And what will your answer be then?"

"I don't know, Mother—I'm as confused and disturbed as you are." Livy lifted the manuscript and held it in both hands. "I've never met a man like Mark before—I suppose no one has. I agree with Father about his brilliant mind. And ever since I've known him he's awakened *my* mind. I admire him and respect him because—well—he's *illuminated* my life."

Olivia gave a tiny gasp. "Oh? In that case do you think you *could* reject a proposal of marriage?"

Livy lowered her voice. "I think so—if only in fairness to Mark."

"Fairness?"

"Yes. His life is strenuous and exciting and always will be. The woman he marries will need an endless supply of strength to match his own. And," she added with a trace of bitterness, "as you've pointed out so often, I'm not so fortunately endowed."

"That's true, dear, and I'm glad you realize it." Olivia cleared her throat. "One more thing if you don't mind. Have you told Mr. Clemens about your serious illness as a child?"

"No, Mother, up to this point I've had no reason to tell him."

Olivia's lips narrowed. "But since you insist upon fairness, don't you think . . . ?"

"Oh, Miss Livy," Barney interrupted as he came through the door. "I see you're still on the job."

"Barney," Olivia began, but her voice was too faint to be heard.

He dropped several pages of manuscript on the table at Livy's elbow. "Got a message from Mark. He says to give you this next chapter right away, so's you can start cuttin' out all the good, juicy parts." He winked at Olivia. "That man's a caution, ain't he, Mrs. Langdon?"

Livy pulled her chair close to the table and picked up her pencil. "Thank you, Barney," she said purposefully. "I'll get busy right away, before he gets too far ahead of me."

Barney touched his forehead and headed for the carriage house. Olivia turned to resume the conversation with her daughter, but saw that Livy was already at work. With a sigh and a shake of her head, she left the summer house and made her way up the path toward the main house and the comfortable security of her room.

9

ON the eighth morning of his convalescence, Mark put on his clothes and joined the family in the breakfast room. All the Langdons, including Charlie, were pleased to see him moving about again.

"Welcome back to the living, Mr. Clemens," Jervis said jovially. "I sincerely hope you are feeling as well as you look."

"Thank you, sir, I feel as strong as a horse," Mark replied, and added quickly, "Maybe not as strong as *your* horse, but certainly equal to the ordinary, run-of-the-mill cayuse."

"Bessie has always been so gentle," Olivia said, looking puzzled. "I simply cannot understand what made her so skittish that night."

"Neither can I, Mrs. Langdon," Mark said, "unless she was worried about my missing the train."

Charlie swallowed a piece of beefsteak and spoke half seriously. "You're not going to sue Father for the accident, are you, Mark?"

"No, Charlie, that would only start a whole round of

legal bickering. If I sued him for the dent in my head, he'd sue me right back for the dent in his driveway."

Jervis shook with laughter, almost upsetting his coffee cup. "That's rich, really rich. I must remember to tell that one at one of our club dinners."

The week passed quickly, and Livy and Mark spent many of the daylight hours working together in the summer house. Leave-taking was difficult for both of them, and Mark departed with an invitation to return whenever his schedule made it possible.

During a stay in Hartford, where he inquired into the progress of his book, Mark lived with his editor Elisha Bliss. Mrs. Bliss, a gentle, kindly woman, introduced him into the social life of her group, and he spent many pleasant evenings with the Blisses' friends and neighbors, particularly those who were members of the Asylum Hill Congregational Church. Owing to the fact that the majority of the male members were tremendously prosperous in business, Mark dubbed their house of worship the "Church of the Holy Speculators."

It was this church connection that led to Mark's meeting its pastor, Joseph Hopkins Twichell, a man of his own age, soon to become his closest and dearest friend. When "Joe" Twichell invited him into his home to meet his young wife Harmony, Mark expressed his admiration of their peaceful, happy existence and told them of his love for Livy Langdon. "I haven't yet asked her to marry me," he said, "and she really oughtn't to marry me. But whether she does or doesn't,

I shall be sure that the best thing I ever did was to fall in love with her, and proud to have it known that I tried to win her."

A short while later, in Boston, Mark signed a contract with James Redpath of the Boston Lyceum Bureau, the best lecture agency in the business, and set out on a tour that brought him an income almost commensurate with his fame. His new lecture, "The Vandal Abroad," based upon the *Quaker City* letters, was so well received that he quickly became the most popular speaker on the platform circuits.

One golden autumn day, with time on his hands and loneliness in his heart, Mark took a side trip to Hannibal, Missouri, the slumbering river town in which he had spent so much of his boyhood. Noting that his old home on Hill Street looked a little smaller than he remembered it and that everything else seemed to have changed somewhat over the years, he strolled down the hill after breakfast to have a sentimental look at the river. Hearing young voices at the water's edge, he walked quietly to the end of the footpath, spied two boys of ten or eleven, one black and one white, and stopped a moment to observe them and listen to their conversation.

The white boy lay on the bank with a straw hat pulled down over his eyes. A store-bought fishing rod was propped up between two rocks, its line dangling in the water. The other boy was standing knee-deep in the river, bending over to capture a small nail keg as it floated toward him in the slight shore current. As Mark watched, the idle boy slapped at something that was apparently crawling on his chest, then sat up suddenly and captured the crawler with a sweep of his cupped hand.

Peeking into his closed fist to see what he had caught, he called excitedly to his friend, "Hey, Cat! Cat!"

The other boy tossed the keg up on the bank. "Yeah, Henry? What?"

"C'mere, quick—look what I got!"

Cat came running. "You ketch a fish?"

"No, a bug—look." Henry opened his fist slightly, and Cat peered in and whistled.

"You know somethin', Henry? That's the biggest bug I ever see. What you goin' to do with him?"

"Chuck him in the river and find out if he can swim." Henry tossed the bug into the water, and at once a fish's mouth broke the surface and the bug was gone.

"Oops," Cat exclaimed, "now we'll never find out."

"Good morning, boys," Mark called. The youngsters jerked their heads around as Mark came down and joined them. "Caught anything?"

"Only a big black bug," Henry said.

"Yeah," said Cat, "and a big black catfish caught *him.*"

"Too bad you didn't have the bug on your hook," Mark said.

"Henry's fishin' in the wrong pool," Cat told him. He pointed downriver. "Best cats in the Mississippi hang around down yonder."

"Aa, they do not," Henry argued. "Ain't a better pool'n this one on the whole river."

"Mine's better," Cat insisted. "If it ain't, then why do you reckon folks call me Cat?" He looked up at Mark. "I catch more fish'n anybody."

"You don't say?" Mark pointed upriver. "Since you boys are arguing about catfish pools, the best one of all is fifty yards up that way."

"How do you know?" Henry asked.

"Because I used to fish there."

"When?"

"A long time ago."

"That pool used to be good, mister," Cat said, "but it ain't the same no more. Now it's all filled up with junk."

Mark pursed his lips. "Well, as I said—it was a long time ago." He pointed to Henry's fishing gear. "That's a fine-looking rod you've got there, Henry."

"Yes, sir, I got it for my birthday."

"I got a good one, too," Cat said proudly. "It's propped up down there in *my* pool."

"You boys are lucky," Mark said. "All I ever had was a stick, a string, and a bent pin."

Cat wrinkled his nose. "Fishin' ain't the same no more. That's the ole-fashion way."

"Maybe so, but I was an old-fashioned boy." Shading

his eyes, Mark looked up and down the broad water-way. "I even thought this river was something wonder-ful. It seemed like a broad highway to the sea and the whole world beyond."

Henry's interest perked up. "You ever been down-river, mister? I mean all the way to New Orleans?"

"Oh, yes, quite a few times."

"That really must be somethin'," Cat said dreamily. "I'm goin' to take me down to New Orleans someday for sure."

Henry frowned. "Who said so?"

Cat grinned. "Abr'm Lincoln."

"Another old-fashioned thing we boys used to do," Mark told them, "was float a raft over to the island and hunt for turtle eggs."

"How?" Cat asked.

"Well, what we did was poke a long stick way down in the mud, and when we hit something soft, we dug down with our hands. Sometimes we'd find fifty, maybe sixty eggs in one hole."

"Gol-lee!" Henry said. "That'd be fun."

"Oh, we had plenty of fun way back in those prehis-toric times. We'd hunt for squirrels and partridges by day and coons and possums by night."

"Possums," Cat said, rubbing his stomach. "Mm-*mm!*"

"We were always on the move," Mark said, pointing north, then south, "from Holliday's Hill down to McDowell's Cave." He nodded his head toward mid-river. "You boys ever swim across to Glasscock's Island?"

Henry scowled. "Swim? Uh-uh. How far is it?"

"Well, it *used* to be half a mile."

Henry's rod was jerked suddenly. "Hey, I got a bite!"

"Maybe I got one, too," Cat shouted, running down the bank. "I'll go see."

Henry reeled in a middle-size catfish. "Boy, lookit him! Cat won't ever catch one even half as big as this, I bet."

Mark nodded. "That's a pretty nice fish, Henry."

Henry laughed. "See? I told you no pool's better'n this one."

"Wow-ee! Oh, man!" Cat was heard shouting.

"What happened?" Henry yelled.

"Wait'll you see!" Cat raced toward them with a giant catfish squirming at the end of his line. "Lookit what *I* caught!"

"Boy!" Henry said enviously.

Cat was elated. "Ain't he a big son of a gun?" He grinned up at Mark. "See, mister, didn't I tell you my pool's best?"

"Yes, Cat, you sure did."

"Hey, Cat," Henry said, "let's take 'em up to my house and fry 'em."

"Yeah, come on!"

"Wait," Mark said. "Why not build a fire right here and cook them on the rocks?"

"What for?" Cat asked.

125

"Well—that's what *we* boys used to do . . ."

Henry cut in. "It's easier at my house. We got a stove and a fryin' pan." Grabbing his fish and gear, he ran up the path. "C'mon, Cat, I'll race you as far as Hickey's Barn!"

Cat sped after him. "When *I* get there, I'll tell Hickey you'll be along next Tuesday."

Mark watched the boys out of sight, then smiled wanly and shook his head. Drawing out his pocket handkerchief, he knelt and dipped it into the water and let the drops fall into his other hand. "Well, anyway," he said in a half whisper, "the river still *feels* the same."

10

TRUE to his promise, Mark dropped in on the Langdons whenever his lecture engagements took him to
New York points not far from Elmira. On a Tuesday
late in November, following vastly successful appearances in Cleveland and Pittsburgh, he arrived at the
Langdon home early in the morning. "The calf has returned," he announced with mock humility. "May the
prodigal have some breakfast?"

Livy and her father were always delighted to see
Mark again; her mother was still not quite certain how
she felt about his visits; and Charlie grumbled a great
deal while still admiring him for his fame and accom-
plishments.

On Thursday, Jervis Langdon invited Mark to be his
guest at his club dinner the following night.

"Livy tells me you're leaving us on Saturday, Mr.
Clemens, so I'd be honored to have you accompany
me." The dinner was a monthly affair, he explained,
and many of Elmira's leading citizens would be in at-
tendance. "Some of them will make speeches after-

wards," he added, "but they're usually quite short, so I don't think you'll be too bored."

"On the contrary," Mark said. "Since words are my stock in trade, I'm always interested in hearing how other men lump them together in public. I'm grateful to you for the invitation and accept with pleasure."

The following morning, when Langdon made his guest's reservation at the club, the word spread quickly around town that Mark Twain was to be present. As a consequence, half an hour before dinnertime the building was crowded with a high percentage of the membership. It was plain that Mark was the lion of the affair, for the men swarmed about Langdon asking to be introduced to the celebrated author and speaker. Mark shook their hands warmly and flattered them by remembering their names throughout the evening.

When the speechmaking began after dinner, Mark paid polite attention, chuckling, nodding, and applauding when it seemed fit to do so.

"I hope it isn't getting too tedious," Jervis whispered during one of the more lengthy talks.

"Not at all," Mark replied. "I'm having a right good time listening to other fellows talk for a change."

The speaker ground slowly to a halt and sat down amid a smattering of applause. A short time later a hush settled upon the room, and all heads turned toward Jervis Langdon, who rose to his feet and glanced guiltily down at Mark. "The tedium is over now, Mr. Clemens," he said in a low voice. "Please forgive me, but I'm about to call upon you for a few words."

Mark was genuinely surprised. "Well, I'll be jiggered," he exclaimed.

When Mark Twain was introduced, he received a standing ovation. Feigning embarrassment and confusion, a trick he always employed when assembling his thoughts, he leaned over the table, fumbling with the water glass, salt cellar, and coffee cup. Straightening up after a moment, he lowered his chin and peered out from under his brows at the expectant guests, turning his head slowly from one side of the room to the other. Shrewdly sensing an imminent explosion of laughter, he delayed it by saluting his listeners with one loud, commanding word: "Gentlemen!" Dropping his voice, he drawled, almost confidentially, "And that's a loose term I always employ when addressing an unfamiliar audience. . . . (Laughter) When I accepted Mr. Langdon's flattering invitation to accompany him here this evening, I hadn't the faintest notion I was going to be called upon to dispense my own particular brand of wisdom. (Laughter) To tell you the truth, I thought it was just an offer of a free dinner, so I pounced on it before he had a chance to change his mind."

A tumult of laughter followed, and the crafty speaker knew that the audience was his for as long as he chose to speak. He glanced down at his beaming host. "Mr. Langdon, why didn't you warn me that I was supposed to make a speech?"

"I suppose I should have," Jervis replied, "but I decided not to burden you with the labor of preparing a formal address."

Mark nodded. "A thrifty decision that will benefit this club's treasury. Whenever I have to work on a lecture ahead of time, I charge a hundred dollars."

From that moment until he resumed his seat, his speech was punctuated with applause and immoderate laughter. Not having memorized his remarks, as he always did for the lecture platform, his mind and tongue were free to roam in all directions. "But I know you wouldn't worry about a hundred dollars," he continued. "It occurs to me that a hundred is small potatoes to this group. Before we sat down to dinner, Mr. Langdon introduced me to a number of you, and I must admit I've never had the chance to meet so many board chairmen and bank presidents. Every time I shook a new hand I could feel that delicious tingle of solid opulence running straight up my arm. (Laughter) The sheer elegance of these premises intimidated me the minute I walked through the front door. Even the lobby has a distinctive aroma—that odor of sanctity that comes with cash."

Later on Mark spoke directly to Thomas K. Beecher, pastor of the church attended by the Langdon family. He told him that Thomas K.'s famous Brooklyn brother, Henry Ward Beecher, had been one of the reasons why Mark had decided to apply for passage on the Holy Land voyage of the *Quaker City*. Mark had wanted to bask in the reflection of the great man's eminence, but at the last moment Henry Ward had canceled his reservation.

"That was a mighty big disappointment for me,"

130

Mark declared, "for it deprived me of the comradeship of an illustrious clergyman and preacher. The story has been circulated that I don't think much of preachers, but that's not strictly true. I have a great fondness for some of them—those I can chin and swap lies with."

Mark then confessed that there was one clergyman among the ship's passengers whom he detested with a vengeance. "The man's ignorance," he said, "covered the entire earth like a blanket, and there was hardly a hole in it anywhere."

Further on, with a wink at his host, he changed smoothly to the subject of bankers, capping his remarks about them with his pet definition of a banker—the borrowed umbrella joke so dear to Jervis Langdon's heart.

Switching to his experiences in Washington, D.C., Mark fired several broadsides at politicians, Congress-men in particular, wrapping it all up with the state-ment: "It could probably be shown by facts and figures that there is no distinctly native American criminal class except Congress."

In concluding his remarks, he announced that so great was his respect for Elmira and its citizens, he had a suggestion to make that, if accepted, would bring to the city the world-wide fame it so justly deserved. His proposal was to erect in the center of Elmira a monu-ment to Adam, the progenitor of the human race. Poor Adam, he reminded them gravely, had never received the recognition he deserved and would soon be forgot-ten; therefore, the monument to his memory should be financed and built without delay. "For a project like this," Mark observed, "somebody always gets stuck with the drudgery of raising funds, so as a temporary loafer here in town, with no duties to speak of and very little cash, I volunteer to accept money." Inviting contributors to file past his table and leave money, in large denominations only, he apologized for having monopolized so much of their valuable time and sat down.

Roaring their approval, the members rushed forward to shake Mark's hand, and the most remarkable event in the club's history came to an end.

When Jervis and Mark returned home, Jervis was still elated by the success of the evening. "Now, Mr. Clemens," he said, "since you're leaving Elmira in the morning, please don't stand on ceremony. The evening is still young, but if you'd like to go straight upstairs to bed, none of us will be offended."

"Thank you, sir," Mark replied, "but I'd like to rest down here for a while and give my stomach a chance to work on that elegant dinner."

"Just as you say." He grasped Mark's arm. "By the way, I hope you didn't mind my dragging you off to that affair. Very often those evenings at the club turn out to be dull."

"I know what you mean, Mr. Langdon, but I enjoyed showing off and felt honored to be included."

"On the contrary, you honored us members by your wit and presence. It isn't often we're able to entertain a celebrated visitor."

They were about to seat themselves when Livy came downstairs, followed by Charlie. "Well, she said gaily, "I see you're back. How was the dinner?"

"Sumptuous," Mark told her. "I'll never be hungry again—unless I'm faced with eating my own cooking."

Charlie noticed Mark's dress clothes. "Say, where'd you get these fancy duds? You never wore those on the *Quaker City*."

"No, Charlie, I didn't. This clawhammer coat is usually reserved for club dinners and speechmaking."

"Did you make a speech tonight, Mark?" Livy asked.

"Yes, I got up on my hind legs and delivered a short, instructive sermon."

Jervis chuckled reminiscently. "I really wish you two young people had been there. I've never heard such loud laughter in that old dining room."

"Father told me he was going to call on you," Livy confessed, "but he made me promise not to tell. Were you very surprised?"

"Flabbergasted. When I heard him announce my name, I almost swallowed my spoon."

"Did you say anything about the *Quaker City?*" Charlie asked.

"Yes I did, among other things."

"Some of his droll comments even made Thomas K. Beecher laugh," Jervis said.

Mark frowned. "I didn't say anything to offend the Reverend, did I, Mr. Langdon?"

"No, but you might have wounded several of our

bankers with your umbrella joke." Jervis grinned. "Served them right if you did; some of them are fairly stuffy."

"Gosh, Mark," Charlie said, "did you really have the nerve to tell the umbrella joke?"

"I'm afraid I did, Charlie. I hope the bankers don't gallop out here tonight with tar and feathers."

"What is the umbrella joke?" Livy asked.

"It's Mr. Clemens's definition of a banker," her father explained. He turned to Mark. "How does it go again? A banker is a man who lends you an umbrella when it starts to rain and—"

"No—when the sun's shining."

"Oh, of course, when the sun's shining, and demands it back the minute it starts to rain. Ha! That's rich, really rich."

Charlie snorted. "Huh—things have certainly changed around here. I thought you said we'd never repeat that joke in Elmira."

"I did, but I never said anything about Mr. Clemens repeating it."

Charlie colored awkwardly. "No, sir, I guess you didn't." Turning, he raced up the stairs, two at a time. "Excuse me," he called back. "I'll go in and say good night to Mother."

"Has she retired?"

"Yes, sir, about an hour ago."

Jervis looked at his pocket watch. "Livy, if you and Mr. Clemens will pardon me, I'll go up and read to your mother for a few moments before she goes to sleep."

"Very well, Father." After he had gone, Livy looked at Mark and shook her head. "I just don't understand what's gotten into Charlie; he's been acting so sullen lately."

"It's only a temporary lapse, I'm sure. I have a hunch he'll recover very soon now."

"But he's almost rude, and that isn't at all like him. But let's not think of Charlie for a while, Mark." She picked up some manuscript pages from a table. "Before Father comes back, I'd like to talk about this new chapter you gave me to read this afternoon."

Mark pulled a long face. "You sound ominous—is it that bad?"

"No, Mark, as a matter of fact, I think it's the best one you've written so far."

He brightened. "Well now, that's high praise. No editorial improvements?"

"Only a few suggestions. I've written them in the margins." They sat together on the divan. "Here, take these pages and look them over."

He waved them away. "No thanks. I'll mail them to my publisher sight unseen."

"But you mustn't do that," she said firmly. "*The Innocents* is *your* book."

"Not any more. I mine the ore, Livy, but you refine it. And among more important things, you've taught me not to confuse 'who' with 'whom,' and shown me

when 'you and I' should win out over 'you and me.' "
She smiled. "So if the book should turn out to be a success, half the credit will be owed to Miss Livy Langdon, Lady Editor of Elmira, New York."

"Oh, Mark, please be serious."

"But it's true. My publisher has already noted the absence of impurities in the chapters I've sent him during the past two weeks. He's gleeful about my reformation and suspects that I've taken holy orders."

"Now you're teasing me."

"No, really, I had a letter from Bliss only last week. He complimented me upon what he called 'the perceptive editing and surprising refinements' that he found in my recent copy." He looked at her soberly. "So now, honored sister, do you understand why I value your changes in my manuscript?"

"But surely you don't agree with all of them," Livy persisted.

"No, I must admit I don't. To tell you the honest truth, you prune away every salty phrase that sounds good to me." His eyes danced. "Actually, Livy, I believe you're steadily weakening the English tongue."

"Now I know you're teasing. But be serious, Mark. I think you should write to please yourself, not me or your publisher."

"I get my pleasure in correcting your spelling. You're a first-class editor, Livy, but a natural misspeller."

"What? You know that isn't true."

"All right, missy, I'll test you. Let me hear you spell 'scissors.' "

"That's an easy one." She frowned and spoke the letters haltingly: "C-i-s-s-e-r-s."

Mark roared and threw his hands up. "Jumping Jehoshaphat! The minute I land in New York tomorrow I'm going to send you a dictionary."

"Thank you. I promise to consult it whenever I'm in doubt." Looking directly into his eyes, she added solemnly, "We're going to miss you, Mark, after you've gone."

He punched the cushion with his fist. "Confound it, Livy, stop that!"

"Stop what?"

"Looking at me that way—stop it!" She drew back, startled. "Not on my last night with you—it isn't fair." He sprang up and began pacing back and forth. "This isn't the place—and there's not enough time!"

Livy was astounded by his vehemence. "Mark, what *are* you talking about?"

"You know blamed well what I'm talking about. Why didn't you look at me that way yesterday—or the day I arrived? Then I could have prepared you for this and led up to it leisurely and properly." His voice grew in volume. "But tonight, with time as my enemy, it's got to come as an explosion!"

She glanced anxiously up the staircase and made a warning gesture. "Sh! Sh!"

Mark stopped pacing and leaned down above her. "I love you and you know it!" Her eyes widened as he shook his finger close to her nose. "Don't deny that you know it, either!"

"I do know it, Mark," she said simply.

"All right then." He sat beside her and spoke gently, pleadingly. "Livy, I can't think it possible that you'd marry me—but will you?" She looked at him incredulously. "Will you, my dearest, will you?"

Frightened by his ardor, she looked down at her trembling hands. "I don't know the answer to that, Mark."

"Then tell me this—do you have any fondness for *me?*"

"That's evident—isn't it?"

He spread his palms out. "Well then, surely you *do* know the answer."

Livy's face clouded as she rose to her feet. "Mark, look at me. Do you see any strength in my body? I mean any equal to yours?"

"I see only a lovely, dignified young woman, Livy."

"But a delicate, terribly frail one." She sat beside him again. "Now, Mark, I must tell you something about myself, so please listen quietly." In a low, almost toneless voice she told him about her skating accident six years earlier, her two years as an invalid, and her agonizing period of convalescence. "Finally I was able to move again, and my health improved steadily. Now I'm twenty-two and apparently sound, but fatigue and exhaustion always come quickly. And so, Mark," she concluded huskily, "I suppose I do know the answer after all."

Mark shook his head vigorously. "Livy, I've asked

138

you to be my wife, but you turned me down. I will not accept a rejection based upon physiological anxiety. You'd be a matchless partner for me, and if you need strength to share my life, I'll supply it in good measure." He gave her a sidelong glance. "However, I suspect that your health isn't the true reason for your refusal to marry me."

"What?" she exclaimed, taken aback.

"I suggest that it's your fear of family opposition."

"Mark!"

He raised a silencing hand. "Charlie told me long ago about your near-canonization by this household. And unless they're all blind, they know that I'm deeply in love with you." Bitterness crept into his tone. "But clearly they've decided that this rough diamond from the West is no fit match for their perfect pearl of the East." He fixed her with his eyes. "Well, what do you say to that?"

"I wouldn't have put it that bluntly," she replied, her small chin jutting forward.

"Then I'm right," he said, almost triumphantly. "You've already received instructions to repel the uncouth invader."

"That isn't true! No one has given me instructions of any kind."

"Ah, but just wait," he insisted. "When the storm breaks, they will. Your father has a liking for me, I think, but wouldn't fancy me as a son-in-law. As for your gentle mother—I reckon I frighten her more than anything else. And Charlie—well, he's kicking himself for having invited me here in the first place. But I love you with all my heart, Livy—and I'm not going to lose you just because you're afraid of your family."

"I'm *not* afraid of my family—I'm *not!*"

"But they're afraid of *me,* Livy, and there lies the dilemma. So it appears there's nothing left for me to do but change my character." He adopted a mocking tone. "Let's see now—do you think they'd open their arms to me if I sprinkled my head with ashes, rent my garments, and promised to be pious and righteous till death do us part?" Leaping to his feet, he hurried to the staircase. "By golly, that's an idea! I think I'll go up and propose that to them."

Livy ran to him and clutched his arm. "No, Mark, please—they wouldn't understand."

He paused, studying her face. "I was right—you *are* afraid of your family."

"I'm not!"

"Sure you are," he scoffed. "You're Papa's obedient, fainthearted little girl."

She covered her ears. "Stop it, stop it! I won't listen!"

Glancing upward, Mark saw Jervis Langdon descending the stairs. "All right then—have you courage enough to let me speak to your father?"

"Speak to me about what?" said Jervis.

Livy swung around, startled, as Mark addressed her father. "Your daughter admits she's fond of me, Mr. Langdon, but won't consent to marry me."

140

Langdon glanced at Livy and sighed. "So it's finally come to a head, has it, Mr. Clemens?"

"Yes, sir, and not unforeseen, I judge."

"No, of course not. My wife and I have been expecting this encounter."

"Then let's come to grips. Livy has refused my proposal for a reason that fails to convince me. I suggested that it's because she fears parental opposition."

Jervis stiffened. "Oh?" To Livy he said, "And *do* you fear our opposition?"

"I don't fear it, Father, but I know it exists."

"Well, now," he muttered, tugging at his beard. "Well, well—yes—hm."

"I'll be gone in the morning," Mark resumed. "So would you favor me now with a moment or two for discussion?"

"It has to be now," Jervis said. "Livy, I'm sure you'd like to go up and bid your mother good night."

"Very well, Father." To Mark she added pleadingly, "No ashes—promise?"

He grinned and crossed his heart. "I promise."

With a troubled glance at Mark, she started up the steps. The men watched her until she vanished down the hall, then took chairs, side by side.

"What was that about ashes?" Jervis inquired curiously.

Mark shrugged. "A small joke of no consequence." Without thinking, he drew out a cigar.

"Something to do with smoking, perhaps?" Jervis suggested pointedly.

With a wry smile, Mark returned the cigar to his pocket. "Sorry, Mr. Langdon. I guess that's a poor way to open this pow-wow."

"We have certain prejudices in this house. Not many, but a few." Clearing his throat, he adopted an official-sounding tone. "Now then, Mr. Clemens, let's get down to it. First of all let me assure you I'm convinced that you love my daughter, deeply and sincerely."

"I'd lay down my life for her."

"I believe you." He frowned. "The crux of the matter is her feeling for you. If she doesn't return your love, this discussion is pointless. What was her reaction to your proposal?"

Mark pursed his lips. "Well, sir, I wish I could tell you that she threw herself into my arms at that moment, but she didn't."

"What did she do?"

"She looked scared. And that didn't seem normal to me somehow. I've always held the notion that the answer to the question 'Will you marry me?' is either 'yes' or 'no.' "

Jervis shook his head. "I don't think it's ever that simple, Mr. Clemens."

"Maybe not," Mark admitted. "I guess I've been reading the wrong novels. However, when she recovered from her shock, she did give me an answer, but it wasn't very elucidating. She said, 'I don't know.' "

"But later she refused you for a reason that you thought unconvincing?"

"Yes, she seems to be abnormally concerned about her health."

"Not without reason, I assure you," Jervis said solemnly. "I gather she told you about her illness as a child. Is that correct?"

"Yes, but inasmuch as her health has been restored, I think she should cast the subject from her mind."

Jervis spoke sharply. "Possibly you don't realize, Mr. Clemens, that the girl's illness was very grave indeed. She was completely incapacitated for a long period of time."

Mark made a gesture of annoyance. "Mr. Langdon, when I was a youngster I had measles, mumps, chicken pox, and even the epizootics. If I could outlast those infirmities, Livy can certainly survive a fall on the ice."

Langdon's face flushed. "But, my dear sir, you don't realize the seriousness of—"

"I do realize it," Mark interrupted, raising his voice. "And I think it's high time you stopped dwelling on it and began treating your daughter as a healthy human being."

"But the poor child isn't healthy," her father insisted.

"She could be and *will* be the moment she's no longer considered your 'poor child.' Too much family protection is no less harmful than too little."

"Well now," Jervis said sardonically, "it never occurred to me that our man-to-man discussion would develop into a lecture on psychology."

"I'm fighting for my future, Mr. Langdon," Mark

143

argued. "And since the odds are against me, I've got to use every weapon in the armory."

"The odds being Livy's so-called fear of opposition by her family?"

"Exactly, and that opposition is real, I'm sure. Doubtless you've thought about losing your daughter in marriage some day, but certainly not to a man like me."

Langdon managed a slight smile. "Having lived all my life in Elmira, Mr. Clemens, I've never even visualized a man like you. Our backgrounds, you must admit, are somewhat dissimilar."

"That's true," Mark admitted. "I had the disadvantage of being born into an impecunious family."

"A disadvantage that you and I happen to share. Owing to my father's desperate financial situation, I left school and became a shop clerk at the age of fifteen."

Mark glanced appraisingly at the room and its furnishings. "Well, sir, you must have been an uncommonly good clerk, judging by these practical results. I'd be satisfied to do about one-eighth as well."

With the new subject, Langdon felt more at ease. "Just what are your financial prospects, Mr. Clemens?"

Mark stretched his legs out and studied the ceiling. "My prospects? Well, let's see—I'd call them modest but promising. With my new lecture I'm earning a hundred dollars or more each night it's delivered, and that's about three nights a week." Langdon raised his eyebrows in approval as Mark continued. "And my new book, if it does well, should bring a nice addition to the kitty."

"That's indefinite, however."

"Right. My bank account won't ever run ahead of yours, I'm afraid, but if Livy were to become my wife, I assure you she'd never want for a blessed thing."

"I should hope not," Jervis said flatly. "Now, as to your future manner of earning a living—have you considered that at all?"

"I have, sir, at great length. Truthfully, I've no ambition to become a professional author. But I've always had a liking for the newspaper business, so after this book's published, I plan to buy into a newspaper and have a nice comfortable income."

Langdon nodded his approval. "And of course you'd give up your lecturing."

"Hardly," Mark answered quickly. "That's too ripe a plum to throw away. If the book's a success, my lecture fees are bound to grow, and I'll be in wider demand for engagements all over the country."

"In that case you'd be away from home a good deal of the time."

"Yes, but I wouldn't mind because Livy could always go along with me to share the fun."

Langdon's face clouded. "Are you serious? Livy could never withstand the rigors of that kind of life."

"I disagree," Mark retorted. "With a joy and excitement that she'd never known before, Livy would flourish."

"Never! I know the girl's capacities far better than you do!"

"Our 'poor child' again, Mr. Langdon?"

"Our *beloved* child, Mr. Clemens."

Mark threw his hands up wearily. "Well, I guess I've failed to make my point about the hazards of too much family protection."

"A belabored point, my friend. Livy is our daughter, and our only concern is for her physical well-being."

Mark snorted. "And to hell with her happiness."

"Clemens!"

Mark ignored the rebuke, his temper aroused. "You don't want a contented, vigorous woman, Mr. Langdon —what you want is a hothouse flower. Keep her a spinster, or marry her to some god-damned Elmira pipsqueak, and that's exactly what you'll get!"

"Clemens," Langdon hissed, deeply shocked, "I find your language both obnoxious and offensive."

"Yes, sir, I reckon you do. But don't expect me to apologize, because I speak and write the language of the human animal." Leaping to his feet, Mark began to pace back and forth, talking as he moved, gesticulating to drive his points home. Langdon listened in silent astonishment, following Mark with his eyes as he moved from one wall to the other like a nervous cat, speaking with his piercing drawl. "I've been a journeyman printer, Mr. Langdon, and a steamboat pilot on the Mississippi on the run from St. Louis to New Orleans. I was a soldier in Missouri for a short spell and a pocket-miner in the raw West for a somewhat longer time. I shoveled silver-tailings in a quartz mill and spent four years as a newspaperman in Nevada and California. During those years I learned the language of the human animal, and today I use it constantly and without shame in all of its magnificent clarity."

Mark kicked a small footstool out of his path and continued his declaration. "Words are my only stock in trade, Mr. Langdon, and when I need to express an idea, the only words I use are those that aim directly at the bull's-eye of my meaning. When the idea itself is obnoxious and offensive, I reject the use of milk-and-water locutions chosen merely for the propitiation of the strait-laced Mrs. Grundy."

Mark stopped at the center of the room and stood facing Langdon. "Therefore, I repeat to you, sir, that if you want your daughter to be a hothouse flower instead of a woman, indulge yourself and marry her to some god-damned Elmira pipsqueak!"

Resuming his seat, he whipped out a cigar, considered it, thought better of lighting it, and returned it to his pocket. Jervis Langdon, struck speechless by Mark's outburst, tiptoed to the staircase and looked up, listening fearfully. "I don't think anyone heard you," he said finally, in a low, conspiratorial tone.

Mark hunched his shoulders. "That's too bad."

Langdon returned to his chair and sat down, regarding Mark with new respect. "Well, Mr. Clemens, shall we get on with the discussion?"

Mark looked at him in astonishment. "You mean my speech didn't kill it dead?"

"No, I thought it was rather admirable, in its way. I haven't heard that kind of oratory since the Republican Convention." He fingered his beard, frowning. "Now let me see—where were we?"

"Nowhere in particular," Mark replied, still looking at the older man incredulously. "I wanted to ask your consent to marry your daughter, but somehow we got sidetracked. So I ask your consent now, Mr. Langdon. Just say yes, and I promise there'll be no further argument."

Jervis raised a cautioning hand. "I suggest you proceed more slowly with this courtship."

"I'm not hurrying my love," Mark protested. "It's my love that's hurrying me."

"But there's much more to be said before any decision can be reached. The truth is, Mr. Clemens, I know very little about you, save the broad, public facts."

"Well, sir, if you want to hear the narrow, private facts, you couldn't have come to a better-informed source. What would you like to know?"

"Well," Langdon began, with a trace of embarrassment, "I hope this won't offend you, but Mrs. Langdon and I are considerably curious about any—uh—shall we say 'foibles' that you might have picked up on the river and in the West."

"Foibles or vices?"

Jervis shrugged. "Call them what you will."

"Well, if you consider smoking a vice, I guess I'm incurably vicious. But I make it a rule never to smoke more than one cigar at a time." Glancing sideways at Jervis, he added apologetically, "That's a stock joke of mine."

"I know—you used it tonight at the dinner. Go on, Mr. Clemens."

"I also drink distilled beverages on occasion, but there I can promise reform. I believe that water, taken in moderation, can't hurt anybody. As for swearing— you already know how I feel about that. In certain trying circumstances, profanity furnishes a relief denied even to prayer."

Langdon's face showed no reaction. "Do you think Livy could adjust herself to your singular philosophy —your dissimilar world?"

Mark's eyes sparkled. "Sir, since your daughter is a wonderful miracle of humanity, I'm sure she'd be able to cope with any situation that ever presented itself. And to give her aid and comfort along the way, she'd have the most adoring husband in history." He waited for a comment, but received none. "But it seems," he continued uncertainly, "that you still question my qualifications to be your son-in-law."

"You're right, Mr. Clemens, I do."

"Then am I to infer"—Mark hesitated, dreading the reply—"that my case is closed?"

"No, merely deferred."

"Oh? For how long?"

149

"Two months at least; possibly even three."

Mark gave a low whistle. "That's a long time to wait. Can you promise a definite decision at the end of that period?"

"If you'll be willing to cooperate; and I'm fairly certain you will."

Mark leaned forward. "Do I smell a proposition in the wind?"

"You may call it that." Langdon's voice softened. "I know the man you are now, Mr. Clemens, and I like you. But I don't know the man you've been. Therefore, in the light of my unawareness, would you consent to submit a list of honorable persons to whom I might write for credentials?"

Mark's eyebrows shot up. "Character witnesses?"

"If that term pleases you." He eyed Mark earnestly. "It's a cold-sounding proposition, but I consider it not unreasonable."

"Well, now," Mark drawled, fascinated by the challenge, "darned if you haven't opened up a whole new can of worms. . . . Hm . . . yes, I'd be willing to furnish you with such a list." He sat back, considering the matter. "You said 'honorable' persons, eh?"

"Yes, people of some present repute who knew you well in the past."

"I see. . . . Hm . . . I don't suppose you'd accept my mother as a reference, would you?"

"Not in this case."

"I don't blame you; that wouldn't be fair. Ma's honorable all right, but too soft-hearted to be believed.

When I was a boy," he went on reminiscently, "her sense of pity was abnormal. She could drown a litter of kittens when she had to, but she always warmed the water first."

Jervis smiled. "Your mother sounds like a splendid woman, but I suggest we return to the subject."

"Oh, yes, the character witnesses. . . . Let's see now. . . . You could write to Joe Goodman, I guess—he was my editor out in Virginia City." Abruptly, he dismissed the thought. "No, that wouldn't be fair, either. I've lied for Joe a hundred times, and he'd lie for me if necessary—so his testimony wouldn't be worth shucks." Mark snapped his fingers. "Say, would you accept preachers?"

"Of course. Did you know any in those days?"

"Dozens of them—the hellfire-and-damnation variety —they wouldn't dare lie." Again he discarded the idea. "On second thought, maybe we'd better forget the preachers."

"Why? You're not losing your confidence, are you?"

"No, sir, just being cautious. But hang it, Mr. Langdon, I've no mortal sins to hide." He jumped up. "I'll go and fetch my address book and have a blue-ribbon list of preachers for you in ten minutes. How'll that be?"

"Excellent. I'll wait here for you."

Mark started up the staircase just as Livy was coming down. She glanced at her father. "Have I come back too soon?"

"No, my dear, I've had my say with Mr. Clemens."

Mark stopped halfway up the flight. "Hang it, Livy —why in tarnation won't your father call me Samuel?"

"I don't know," she replied, taken by surprise. Calling down to her father, she imitated Mark's peevish drawl. "Hang it, Father—why in tarnation *don't* you call him Samuel?"

Noting Jervis Langdon's openmouthed expression of shock and astonishment, Mark laughed uproariously and continued up the stairs.

11

LIVY had been overwhelmed by Mark's furious declaration of love and precipitate proposal of marriage.
Like the other members of her family, she had never
met anyone so brilliant, dazzling, and unorthodox or
even dreamed that such a person existed. That Mark
had awakened her there was no doubt; for the first time
since her illness, someone had given her the assurance
that she possessed sufficient strength to live a normal
life. Although Livy had admitted her fondness for
Mark, he disturbed her to such an extent that she was
not averse to the postponement of their engagement,
agreeing with her father that it was proper that they
learn something of Mark's past before the betrothal
should be officially sanctioned or even considered.

Having presented the names of hellfire-and-damnation preachers, Mark now regretted having made the
list so complete and set out from Elmira tortured by
suspense, realizing that the length of the mail trip to
California precluded receipt of their replies for at least

two months. To make the waiting period more bearable, he flung himself into a feverish program of writing and lecturing.

Night after night, in dreary hotel rooms throughout the East and Middle West, Mark wrote ardent letters to Livy, swearing eternal love and reporting on his progress toward complete reform in thoughts, habits, and deeds. So firm was his resolve to make himself worthy of her own love, the heartsick swain even underwent a period of renunciation of alcohol, tobacco, and bad language.

His awful determination to be regenerated was tested one night in Trenton, New Jersey, when his *Quaker City* shipmates, Dan Slote and Jack Van Nostrand, attended his lecture and came backstage afterward. Mark was pathetically pleased to see faces he recognized, particularly those of his kindred spirits of the Holy Land expedition.

"Jehoshaphat!" he exclaimed. "I can't tell you how downright comforting it is to see you two. Now I won't have to go back to my hotel room and gaze at that seedy print of the Colosseum."

"If you think the Colosseum's bad," Jack said, "you ought to see the rotten picture in our hotel room. I can't decide whether it's Moses dressed as Little Eva or Abe Lincoln draped in a nightshirt."

"Speaking of Moses," said Dan, "Jack claims he's going to sue you for telling that 'Moses who?' story tonight."

"It's a standard part of my new lecture," Mark said. "I tell it about three times a week in different towns, so Jack, if you sue me, you'd better hire a lawyer that doesn't mind traveling." The visitors sat down while Mark changed into a dry shirt. "What're you fellows doing in Trenton?"

"I'm here on business for my father's firm," Dan told him. "And the old man sent Jack along to see that I don't steal too much."

"Sounds like a full-time job, Jack. You must have to watch Dan like a hawk."

"Night and day. I hardly have a chance to steal anything myself."

"How's your busted skull, Mark?" Dan asked. "I read in the paper that your brains leaked out and they put them back with a tablespoon."

"A teaspoon," Mark corrected him modestly. "You know how the papers exaggerate. Anyway, as you can see, I'm all patched up again and twice as mean as I ever was."

"That's mighty mean," Jack said. "How did Charlie Langdon's family stand you all that time you were up there in Elmira sponging off them?"

"Oh, they managed to survive the catastrophe somehow—although they'll probably send me a bill one of these days."

"Didn't they want to throw you out for smoking, or cussing, or carrying-on?"

"I didn't smoke while I was in the main house,"

155

Mark confessed, "but I almost got thrown out once for cussing."

Dan was incredulous. "You didn't *smoke?* What happened? Did you run out of matches?"

"No, the Langdons are Congregationalists. That's the sect that disapproves of smoking unless they're in the tobacco business. Charlie's father sells coal."

Jack spoke up. "What do you mean you almost got thrown out for cussing?"

"Oh, I got mad at Mr. Langdon one night over a microscopic point and let go an oath that almost singed his whiskers. He was pretty riled, but he cooled off after a spell and we parted friends."

"How can a microscopic point make you let go an oath?" Dan asked. "What was the point?"

"Oh, nothing to speak of," Mark answered diffidently. "I just told Mr. Langdon I wanted to marry his daughter, that's all."

Both men evinced surprise. "What?" Dan said. *"You* married?"

"Yep."

"To Charlie's sister?" Jack said.

"Yep, Livy Langdon—Charlie's beautiful, magnificent, excruciatingly indescribable sister."

Dan frowned. "Holy mackerel, that means a wedding present. Now I'll *really* have to steal."

"And I'll have to get a job," Jack added sorrowfully. "Gosh, I sure am sorry I came to Trenton."

"You can both rest easy," Mark assured them seriously. "The wedding may never take place."

"You mean the Langdons insisted you turn Congregationalist and you refused?"

"I'd like to say it was that simple," Mark said, "but it isn't." He put on his hat. "Come on—let's go up to my hotel room and I'll tell you the whole dismal story on the way."

"No, let's go to our room," Jack said. "I want you to tell me whether that picture's Little Eva or Abe Lincoln."

During their walk Mark gave Dan and Jack all the facts, ending with Jervis Langdon's request for character references. "So here I am," he concluded as they entered the room, "waiting in a cold sweat to hear whether I win or lose, according to what the preachers say about me."

Dan sent for some ice and three glasses and brought out a bottle. "That old man Langdon," he mused, "he sounds like a pretty stuffy old bastard."

"Wrong," Mark said, "wrong as can be. He's a very likable man. Just a mite overcautious about his daughter, that's all."

"God Almighty, Mark," Jack said, "if I'd been you, I'd have tucked that girl in my valise and run off with her, leaving a polite note telling her old man to go to hell."

"An interesting sidelight on your character," Mark said, "but I don't want to think about it any more tonight."

Dan had laid out some playing cards and poker chips. "I don't blame you, Mark. Let's play some cards and enjoy ourselves. Here's a box of cigars, fifteen-centers. Help yourself."

Mark put his hand out, then drew it back. "Not now thanks, Dan. Maybe later on."

Dan and Jack exchanged a troubled glance, lighted their own cigars, and remained silent until the cards were dealt and the game began. Within a short time the room was heavy with smoke. From time to time Mark glanced uncomfortably at the box of cigars but remained steadfast. Meanwhile, he lost hand after hand, his mind wandering elsewhere.

"Hey, Mark," Jack said, pulling in a stack of chips, "you haven't poured yourself a drink in that glass. What's wrong? Don't you like Scotch any more?"

"What? Scotch? . . . Oh, sure, Jack, but I'll wait and have one later, if you don't mind."

Jack glanced at Dan again. "Hell no, Mark, I don't mind. But that bump on the head must've done more damage than you thought." He dealt a hand and the betting began.

"Two bits," Mark said, throwing in some chips.

"Raise you two bits," Dan said.

"And two more," said Jack confidently. "Throw in your cards, Mark—I've got you licked."

"Jack," Mark drawled, momentarily attentive, "you were a liar on the *Quaker City,* and you're still a liar." He matched the pot. "See you. Turn 'em over."

Dan whooped as they exposed their hands. "Ha! When will you fellows learn how to play this game?"

He scooped in the chips. "A nice little pile. Much obliged, amateurs."

"Dan," Mark said with a grin, "Jack may still be a liar, but you're still a thief."

"Listen to him," Dan gibed. "Tonight he robbed Trenton of a hundred dollars for that dismal lecture about *our* trip, and he's calling *me* a thief. Deal 'em out, Mark, and no fancy shuffling that you picked up from those crooked river gamblers."

Mark pushed back his chair. "No more poker for me, boys. Count me out—I resign."

"What do you mean?" Jack said. "Don't try to make us believe you're broke."

"No, just frugal. I'm saving up to buy a wedding suit."

"I wouldn't buy it just yet," Dan warned. "I'd hold off till old man Langdon gets those answers back from the West."

Mark's shoulders sagged, and he stared miserably into space. "I sure wish I hadn't put all those preachers on that list. I was a darn fool."

Jack laughed. "A *'darn'* fool? Such language. This must be the new Mark Twain speaking."

"Yeah," Dan said, "no cigars, no booze, and now no cussing. Say, I bet Charlie's sister's trying to reform this old sinner—am I right, Mark?"

Mark looked a trifle abashed. "Well, her letters do suggest that I launder my language a mite. So I'm practicing not to cuss, just to see if I can make it stick."

"But what about the booze?" Jack said. "You haven't had a drink since we got here."

"That's true, but I reckon I can get along without it."

"How angelic! Dan, tell the bellboy to bring up a halo."

"The hell with that," Dan said grimly. "Mark, you bloody hypocrite, if you keep on playing angel like this, so help me I'll throw you out the window." Snatching the bottle up, he sloshed whisky into Mark's glass until it overflowed. "There!" he thundered. "Now drink that down, god dammit!"

Mark's face broke into a huge, relieved grin as he reached eagerly for the glass and raised it to his lips. "Thanks, you diabolic bastard—don't mind if I do."

12

AT the end of January, 1869, during a respite from a fatiguing program of platform engagements, Mark went to St. Louis to spend a few days with his mother. Jane Clemens had not seen him for almost two years, since shortly before the *Quaker City* excursion, and thought, rightly, that he looked a bit peaked. On the evening of his arrival, she cooked him a feast that took two hours to consume, then packed him off to bed just as he was about to fall asleep over his third slice of apple pie.

In the morning, after Mark returned from a walk, he found a note telling him that his mother had gone to the store and would be back shortly. While waiting, he went up to his room to write a letter to Livy.

When Jane returned, she deposited her wraps and parcels and called for her son. "Sam!" No answer. Opening the front door, she called again. "Sam!" Still no answer. "What's gone with that boy, I wonder?" Closing the door, she turned back into the room and screamed at the top of her voice, "Samuel Langhorne Clemens!"

Mark answered from above. "Yes, Ma, I'm coming." He clattered down the narrow staircase. "When a mother or schoolteacher calls a boy by his entire name, it means trouble. What's up, Ma?"

"I could've sworn you'd run off somewhere."

"No, I just got back from my walk and went up to write a letter and fetch a present I brought for you." He handed her a small book. "Here, Ma, this is yours, with all my love."

Jane's face lighted up. "Why thank you, Sammy. Is this another book you wrote?"

"No, I had nothing to do with this one."

"I really liked that frog book you gave me last time you were here. I laughed myself near tearful over it."

"That's nice, but a good many people say this book's even better."

Jane squinted at the small volume over her spectacles. "Why, Sammy, it's a Bible."

"I bought it for you in the Holy Land. Look at the special covers on it. They're different from most—they're olive and balsam wood."

"Fancy that." She turned the book over tenderly, admiring the hand-crafted binding. "It's elegant, just plain elegant."

"Open it and look inside. There's an inscription in it."

"A what?"

"I wrote something in it."

She gave a small gasp. "Sammy! You didn't write anything funny in the *Bible?*"

He gestured impatiently. "Go on, take a look."

Jane turned back the front cover, adjusted her glasses, and read the inscription aloud: "For Jane Lampton Clemens, from her loving son Samuel. Jerusalem, September 24, 1867." Greatly touched, she murmured, "Oh, dear—dearie me."

Mark was pleased. "I've been keeping it for you for more than a year."

She patted his cheek. "Thank you, son, I'll always treasure this Bible and keep it safe. And when I die, you can have it back."

"Ha, you'd better not bank on leaving first, Ma. You'll outstick me for sure."

"You're not ailin', are you?" she asked anxiously, taking a step toward the mantel. " 'Cause if you are . . .'"

He reached out and drew her back. "I know, I know —you've got a new elixir that works like magic."

Her jaw dropped. "Who told you?"

He pointed to the line of medicine bottles. "I looked over your stock this morning while you were rustling up my breakfast."

"But this new one's really powerful, Sammy. You sure you won't take just one spoonful?"

"Nope, I don't need it. I'm feeling as fine as a frog's hair split down the middle."

Jane peered at him suspiciously. "Well, if you're that healthy, how come you laid abed this mornin' till way past seven?"

"Because I'm plumb lazy, that's how come. Early rising never did appeal to me somehow."

"That's a pity, 'cause gettin' up early's the best thing in the world for a person."

"Don't you believe it. I once met a man who got up at sunrise and a horse bit him."

Jane gave his shoulder a gentle jab. "Oh, go on with you and your jokes." Sitting down in her rocker, she reached for her pipe and tobacco. "Last night you told me all about travelin' on the *Quaker City,* but you didn't tell me a single thing about yourself. So, if you feel like it, let's sit a spell and talk." She looked up at him anxiously. "You're not obliged to stand up *this* year, are you?"

"No, thank goodness, my caboose is back to normal." Mark took a chair as his mother lighted her pipe and puffed happily.

"What about your poor head, Sam? You wrote me you were sick abed after you fell out of that wagon up there in New York State."

"That was five months ago. My head was calked up and feels as good as new."

"I was right worried about that accident. It was even in the paper that you were sick."

Mark grinned. "I know. Good news always gets around."

"Tell me the truth, son," Jane said, pointing her pipe-stem at him. "You hadn't been drinkin' that night, had you?"

"I should say not. I was the guest of a respectable temperance family."

She looked relieved. "Well, I'm glad to hear you've got some decent friends back *east.*"

"Back east? What do you mean?"

"To tell you the truth, Sammy, I was always upset about the company you kept out there in San Francisco."

"Some folks are still uneasy about that," he said ruefully. "Tell me something, Ma—are you satisfied I turned out all right?"

"Yes, you seem like a good, decent man to me." She paused, adding, "Maybe not God-fearin', I'm sorry to say, but decent."

He leaned forward. "Any room for improvements, you think?"

"I doubt there's a good person alive that couldn't be even better. Never came across anybody yet that's perfect. Leastways, not here in St. Louis."

Mark looked off into space. "St. Louis isn't the whole world, Ma."

She drew on her pipe until the bowl glowed. "Sam," she said uneasily, "are you sure you're not ailin'?"

"Absolutely, why?"

"You ain't smoked one cigar since you got here."

"That's right," he said sharply.

"Why's that?"

"I'm trying hard not to backslide."

"Well, I'll be. You made up your mind to give up smokin'?"

"Not entirely. I'm just cutting down a little."

"What for?" she asked suspiciously. "Did a doctor tell you to?"

"*No*, Ma, it's my own idea. I thought maybe that might be one of my improvements." Pounding the arm of his chair, he snatched a cigar from his pocket and glared at it angrily. "But I'd sure as hell *like* to smoke you, damn your little brown hide!"

Jane spoke sharply. "If you're truly lookin' to improve, you might cut down on your cussin'."

Mark gestured helplessly. "I'm trying to do that too, Ma, but it comes hard. Without profanity I'm as jumpy as a grasshopper." Jamming the cigar back into his pocket, he strode to the window and stared out. "Right now I'd like to run down to the river and cuss out loud for about three hours and twenty-six minutes!"

She twisted around in her chair. "You got somethin' real worrisome on your mind, Sammy. Don't you want to tell your ma about it?"

He nodded, without turning. "Why do you think I stopped off to see you?"

Jane studied the back of his head. "Well—you goin' to tell me now or after you've done cussin' the river?"

"Now, Ma, right now's the time." Returning to the center of the tiny room, he paced back and forth between the rocker and the mantel. "When I got to Chicago day before yesterday, there was a letter waiting for me. It was from a man named Jervis Langdon, of Elmira, New York."

"Elmira," Jane said reflectively. "Ain't that where you fell out on your head?"

"Yes. Mr. Langdon has summoned me back to Elmira for a momentous discussion that will make me the happiest—or the most miserable—man on earth."

Jane groped through her memory. "Mr. Langdon—I recall him now. He has a boy named Charlie that you met on the boat."

"Ma! You're not listening."

"I am, too. Let's see now," she mused. "You wrote that there's a Mrs. Langdon, and a grown daughter called—Libby."

"Livy, Ma, Livy!"

"Oh, yes, Livy. I remember thinkin' that it's such a pretty name to say out loud."

"Ma, listen." Mark stopped pacing and bent down. "Didn't you hear what I said about that momentous discussion?"

"Sure I did—it's goin' to make you either happy or miserable." She rocked quietly, as though the subject were closed.

"But don't you want to know why?" he asked in exasperation.

Jane stopped rocking. "I reckon I already know why without askin'. You want to marry Mr. Langdon's daughter." Mark appeared dumbfounded as she looked up at him and smiled. "Why else would you want to cut down on your smokin' and cussin'?"

He stared at her for a moment, then his face broke into a broad grin. "Well, I'll be jiggered. You're twice as smart as a bird dog."

"I'm glad you finally found yourself a girl, Sammy."

She reached her hand out. "Now come over here and tell me all about her."

Mark knelt beside her, talking eagerly. "Ma, she's perfect, like—like the person you said you've never yet come across."

"I said not here in St. Louis."

"But in Elmira I found her—and she's Livy Langdon. She's only a little body, but she hasn't her peer in Christendom. She's the dearest girl in the world, Ma, and I'm in love beyond all telling."

Jane patted his head. "It don't need tellin', Sammy —it's as plain as tar on a white cat. Is she in love with you?"

Mark frowned. "I think she is." He leaped up, enthused. "No, by jingo, I know she is."

"But she hasn't come right out and said so?"

He hesitated. "Not directly." His enthusiasm returned. "But we've been writing each other two or three times a week, and her letters are warm with tenderness and understanding."

"Then what's holdin' her back?"

"Her family. They're not sure I'm good enough for her." Jane snorted contemptuously. "Like you, Ma, they're concerned about the company I kept out west, and they've got questions to ask. Mr. Langdon's written to some of my old acquaintances, and their answers have finally come back. I've got nothing to hide about my life out there, but in spite of that I'm scared stiff. When I face Mr. Langdon, I'm going to feel like a prisoner in the dock, awaiting the verdict of the jury."

"Well, son, I feel for you," Jane said, "but on the other hand, I don't see why it should all be one-sided. So there's a question that *your* family wants to ask." She looked at him searchingly. "Is Livy Langdon good enough for *you?*"

Mark chuckled. "You're a wonder, Ma, and that's a fact. My answer is yes—Livy's a thousand times good enough for me. I don't ask you to love her beforehand, but when you meet her, you won't be able to help loving her—even if you try."

Jane stood up. "That satisfies me, Sammy." Reaching into his pocket, she took out the cigar and handed it to him. "Now here—if I was you, I'd backslide just this once and quit fussin'."

Eagerly, Mark struck a match and lighted up. "Thanks, Ma," he said, "don't mind if I do."

13

MARK had settled upon the title of his book with Elisha Bliss. It was to be *The Innocents Abroad or The New Pilgrim's Progress,* a double-barreled appellation that would offend no one, inasmuch as it was believed, and rightly as it turned out, that only the first part would be commonly used.

True to his promise, Mark had sent Livy a dictionary, which she used almost constantly while working on the revised proofs that arrived by post several times each week. Fortunately for Mark, and for his book, Livy's perception, delicacy, and taste refined the text and beautified the manuscript as it came to her for editing.

After spending two days in St. Louis, Mark proceeded to Elmira for his own personal editing, hoping for acceptance but fearing rejection. Shortly after noon, when Barney delivered him to the Langdon home, both Livy and her mother were there to greet him, and, to Mark's annoyance, Olivia Langdon stayed close to him and Livy throughout the afternoon. As though abiding by an unspoken agreement, not a word was said about the chief purpose of Mark's visit. Instead, he entertained the two ladies with a description of his travels and adventures since he had last seen them. Although Olivia was slow at times to comprehend Mark's humor, she was gracious and made him feel welcome.

Late in the afternoon Mark excused himself and asked Barney to drive him downtown for a shave and haircut. About an hour later Charlie came home from his new job with a hardware company and was hanging up his hat and coat just as Livy came downstairs.

"Oh, hello, Charlie. How are you getting along at business?"

He kissed her cheek. "Not fast enough for me, sis. This was my tenth day on the job, and the boss still hasn't offered me a partnership."

"Well, don't be discouraged. Give him one more week—he'll recognize your true worth."

Charlie glanced around the room. "I thought Mark would be here. Didn't he come?"

"Yes, his train was on time for a change. He was here most of the afternoon."

He paused. "Just you and Mark?"

Livy smiled. "No, Charlie, Mother kept us company the entire time."

He seemed slightly abashed. "I was just asking. Where is he, up in his room?"

"No, Barney drove him down to the barbershop. He should be back soon."

Charlie grinned. "With all that hair they ought to charge him double."

"I really think Mark should charge *them*. Barney says he keeps all the men in the shop laughing. He's their most popular customer."

"I guess he is," Charlie said wistfully. "He's popular with everybody."

Livy squeezed his hand. "Mark's terribly anxious to see you, Charlie. He's ever so fond of you."

He brightened. "How do you know?"

"He told me so."

"I'm glad to hear that. You know, I've thought a lot about him since he was here before." He hesitated. "I —I guess you have too, haven't you?"

"Yes, Charlie, a great deal."

He fingered a loose button on his jacket. "Livy."

"Yes?"

"Are you and Mark—I mean—are you going to marry him?"

"Now, Charlie," she said reproachfully, "you know what Father told us. We're not to discuss that subject until Father brings it up himself."

"I know, but—well, even people outside the family have suspicions about it."

"Charlie," she said in amazement, "how could they?"

"I don't know, Livy. I guess the cook, or maybe the maid, has been spreading rumors around town."

"Oh, dear."

"I know Barney suspects. As a matter of fact, he

172

asked me outright this morning when he found out Mark was coming."

"He *did?* What did you tell him?"

"I said it was none of his blamed business. But he just laughed and said, 'Aw, come on now, Charlie, who're you tryin' to fool?'"

Livy clucked her tongue. "If Father knew about that, he'd be furious."

"That's no lie. Tell me something—did you invite Mark to come for this visit?"

"No, Father did."

"I thought so."

"Why?"

"Because he sent a letter to Mark in Chicago last week."

"Who told you that?"

"Barney."

"How did he know?"

"He mailed the letter."

Livy stamped her foot. "Oh, that busybody! I could wring his neck." She had hardly finished speaking when the front door opened and Barney peered in cautiously. She pointed an accusing finger at him. "I want to talk to you."

Barney raised a hand for silence. "Sh—not now."

"But, Barney . . ."

He put a finger to his lips and spoke in a hoarse, conspiratorial whisper. "Tell me, Miss Livy, would your father be back home from his office yet?"

"No, he hasn't come, but why on earth are you whispering?"

" 'Cause if he was back, I didn't want him to hear me askin'."

"Why not?" Charlie said. "Are you afraid to see Father for some reason?"

"No, it's Mark—I mean Mr. Twain—that's afraid to see him. I'll go and tell him the coast is clear."

"Is he outside?" Charlie asked eagerly.

"Yep, walkin' back and forth in the driveway, jumpy as a flea. He told me to peek in and get the lay of the land 'cause he didn't want to bump smack into your father without bein' prepared."

Charlie hurried out the door, calling, "Hey, Mark, what's the idea of hanging around out there?"

"Barney," Livy said in a severe tone, "did Mr. Twain tell you why he's nervous about meeting Father?"

He looked down at his feet. "Well yes, Miss Livy, I got to confess he did. But don't you see," he added defensively, "he had to tell *some*body. And I'm proud to say him and I are pretty close friends."

Livy sighed. "Well, all right, but I must warn you not to repeat any of this to anyone. You hear me, Barney? Don't repeat it to anyone."

Seemingly shocked, Barney drew himself up. "Why, Miss Livy, I'd never dream of doin' such a thing. One thing I'm not is a blabbermouth."

He turned and started out just as Mark and Charlie entered. Mark squeezed his arm. "Thanks for scouting

174

for me, Barney. Charlie tells me I have a short reprieve before my dreaded meeting with his father."

"That's right, Mark. Be sure and leave me know how it turns out, will you?"

"If it doesn't turn out, I might ask you to drop me on my head again."

Barney raised his hands. "God save us from that. Shall I say a prayer for you?"

"If you want to. But be sure to make it clear who you're talking about." Mark pointed heavenward. "I'm not too well known up there."

"Don't you believe it. If his eye is on the sparrow, you can be sure he's noticed you once or twice." Clapping Mark on the shoulder, he stalked out. "Good luck, chum."

Charlie studied Mark's hair appreciatively. "He's all polished up like a dandy, isn't he, sis?"

"I should say so. Your friend the barber did a magnificent job, Mark."

"Thank you, Livy, I even smell good. He doused me with a nickel's worth of heliotrope." He held out his right hand, which shook perceptibly. "But as you can see, it didn't help my nerves any. I should have asked for a sedative instead. Livy, have you told Charlie the reason for my skittish condition?"

"No, Mark, but he must have surmised. He knows Father wrote you asking you to come."

"That's right," Charlie said, "and you just spoke about a dreaded meeting, so I guess it's all pretty plain." He clapped Mark on the shoulder, imitating Barney. "Good luck, chum. I'll say a prayer for you, too." Smiling back over his shoulder, he hurried up the stairs.

Mark grasped Livy's hands. "My dearest darling, is it possible that we're going to be permitted a moment alone?"

"I'm dreadfully sorry about this afternoon," Livy said, "but Mother seemed determined not to let us out of her sight."

He led her to the divan and sat beside her. "Your mother's a fine woman, but she cramps my style considerably." He cleared his throat nervously. "Now, Livy, before your father arrives, tell me—has he given you any hint about the contents of those character letters?"

"No, Youth, not the slightest."

"Well, I wish . . ." He stopped short and swung around. "What did you call me?"

"Youth."

"Say it again."

"Youth." She smiled. "It's a name I invented for you. Do you mind?"

"No, Livy, no, I like the sound of it on your lips." He tried it himself. "Youth . . . hm."

"It seems to fit you somehow—even better than Mark. And I never have liked Samuel much."

"Then Youth I want it to be, forever and ever."

"Youth," she began, "I . . ."

"Lovely, lovely," he murmured.

176

"Youth, tell me something. Why are you so uneasy about those letters?"

"It isn't the letters I dread, my darling. If they should assert that my character is blemished, their statements would be false. But the thought of their causing you distress gives me no peace."

"Would it help if I told you that I have faith in you?"

"Only if it meant that you love me. And that's a declaration you've never made, Livy, either by tongue or pen."

Her eyes softened as she turned to speak. It seemed that she was about to make an admission of her true feelings when her mother appeared from the dining room.

Olivia was startled at finding them alone together. "Why, Mr. Clemens, I had no idea you were back."

"I believe you, Mrs. Langdon," Mark growled, unable to conceal his annoyance.

"Charlie's home too," Livy told her, "but Father hasn't come yet."

"I'm sure he'll be along directly. He told me this morning he'd probably come back earlier than usual." Olivia took a chair close to the divan and smiled placidly. "Now, what have you two been talking about? Have I interrupted you?"

Mark rubbed his chin. "I'm trying to think how George Washington would've answered those questions."

Olivia seemed perplexed. "He's joking, Mother,"

177

Livy said. "Actually, Mark and I were discussing character and faith."

"You were?" Olivia was pleasantly surprised. "Gracious."

"We always tackle the simple subjects first," Mark explained, "before going on to more important things, like the weather."

"Oh, I see." Olivia hesitated, then brightened. "How *was* the weather when you came in, Mr. Clemens?"

"About as everybody expected."

"But—is it turning cooler?"

Mark wrinkled his forehead. "Some people say it is, but that could be just talk. We'll know for sure if the temperature drops."

"Yes," Olivia murmured, looking bewildered, "I suppose we will."

Livy was attempting desperately to catch Mark's eye and put an end to his teasing when the door opened and Jervis Langdon stepped in. "Oh," she said, greatly relieved, "here's Father."

Olivia greeted him. "Hello, Jervis dear."

"Good evening, my pets," he said. "Unseasonably warm outside. Ah, Mr. Clemens, I see you've arrived."

"Yes, sir, the prodigal has returned."

Jervis kissed his wife and daughter and shook Mark's hand. "A pleasure to see you again, Mr. Clemens. Glad you could arrange to come."

"So am I, Mr. Langdon—although my delight is mixed with a large helping of anxiety."

"Anxiety? . . . Oh, yes, of course, I see what you mean." He turned to Olivia. "How soon do you plan to serve dinner, my dear?"

"In about half an hour."

Jervis glanced at Mark. "Shall we dispose of our business now, Mr. Clemens, or wait until after we've dined?"

"Well, sir, if I'm to enjoy the meal, I'd say now."

"As you wish."

"Of course," Mark added, "I may not be able to enjoy it later, either."

"Very well then, come into my study."

"May I come with you, Father?" Livy asked.

"I'd rather you wouldn't, sweetheart. You agree with me, don't you, Mr. Clemens?"

"If I didn't," Mark answered wryly, "I'd be off to a mighty shaky start."

Livy gave him a wan smile. "I'll be waiting right out here, Mark."

Mark blew her a kiss and followed her father into the study. Closing the door, Langdon seated himself in the leather swivel chair, unlocked his desk drawer, and drew out a sheaf of letters. Mark took the chair across the desk, eying the letters uneasily.

"Now then," Jervis began in a businesslike tone, "let's plunge right into this matter. Are you comfortable?"

"No, but let's plunge anyway." Mark mopped his brow and indicated the letters. "Do my friends in the West judge me a saint or a sinner?"

179

"I'll come to that in a moment. First let's consider *my* friends here in Elmira."

Mark scowled, grasping the edge of the desk. "You didn't make it clear that I was to have two sets of judges."

"True, but I've only recently become aware of the local ones." Langdon shook his head. "I was dismayed to learn that your desire to marry my daughter is known to virtually every one of my friends and acquaintances."

"How is that possible? Are they all clairvoyant?"

"How they acquired their knowledge is beside the point, Mr. Clemens. But Elmira is a conservative community, and its citizens hold equally conservative opinions."

Mark lowered his head and peered through his eyebrows. "And they've all turned thumbs down on Clemens?"

"That's the impression I get."

Mark leaped up, roaring. "Well, I'll be damned!"

"You will be," Langdon said sternly, "if you don't quiet down, and *settle* down."

Mark dropped back into his chair, only slightly mollified. "Are you going to permit yourself to be swayed by the puny opinions of these smug, self-appointed critics?"

"Of course I'm not," Langdon snapped. "I make my own judgments."

"I question that."

"On what grounds?"

"On the grounds of these letters." Mark tapped the pile of correspondence. "If you're so all-fired confident of your own judgments, you wouldn't have sought the opinions of *my* friends."

"You don't say." Langdon lowered his voice. "Are you ready to hear their opinions, Mr. Clemens?"

"That's why I'm here." He sat back, tapping the edge of the desk. "Fire away."

"The 'character witnesses,' as you call them, agree unanimously on one point . . ."

Mark cut in: "That my name is Samuel Langhorne Clemens."

Langdon threw down his pen. "If you're determined not to be attentive, we can just as well . . ."

"No, no, I apologize. Resume firing."

"As I was saying, they agree on one point—that you are a brilliant, able man—a man with a future—" Mark smiled and leaned forward—"and that you would make just about the worst husband on record."

Mark slumped back. "Hm—there's nothing very evasive about that."

"I won't read these letters to you in full, but each one contains at least one illuminating statement that you should hear."

"Let there be light," Mark muttered.

Langdon adjusted his pince-nez and picked up the top letter. "This is the opinion of the Reverend Stebbins: 'Clemens is a humbug. I admit he has talent, but will make a trivial use of it.'" He glanced over his lenses, and Mark waved feebly for him to proceed. He

181

referred to the next letter. "The Reverend Scudder: 'Sam Clemens will make his way in the world, I think—but he is altogether shiftless and self-centered.' "

Mark had turned pale and became glassy-eyed as Langdon continued. "Dr. Harlow: 'It seems to me that any woman who married Sam would have to be a long-suffering saint.' " He read the next name in a sepulchral voice. "The Reverend Stone: 'Sam Clemens will make your daughter extremely happy—if he remains a bachelor.' "

Mark's head had telescoped into his shoulders. "Who'd you say wrote that one?"

"The Reverend Stone."

"Let me see that." Mark took the letter gingerly and glanced through it. "Yep, that's what he says, all right." He tossed the letter back. "How many more illuminating statements do you have there?"

"Four or five. Shall I read them to you?"

"All run about the same, do they?"

"In general."

"Then don't bother—I get the drift."

"However," Langdon continued, drawing two letters from the bottom of the pile, "there's a curious coincidence in these last two. They're from Dr. R. B. Swain and the Reverend A. J. Marsh. They agree almost word for word."

"Really?"

"Yes, both men are convinced that you will fill a drunkard's grave."

Mark shook his head. "That's just one of those usual long-distance prophecies. There being no time limit mentioned, there's no telling how long you'd have to wait for it to come true." He heaved a sigh and straightened up. "Well, Mr. Langdon, it looks as if I gave you the wrong list of names. These fellows all make me sound like a typhoid-carrier."

Langdon removed his glasses and rubbed the bridge of his nose. "Haven't you a friend in the world, Clemens?"

"Apparently not."

"I'm not so sure. You have at least one that I know of."

"Who's that?"

"Jervis Langdon."

"*What?*" Mark stared at him incredulously.

"I mean it. I believe in you."

"You do?"

Jervis nodded. "I know you better than all of them. You're a man of enormous integrity and high principle." He beamed. "So you see? I do make my own judgments after all." He reached across the desk. "Welcome— Samuel."

Mark shook the hand and sprang up, overturning his chair. "Livy!" he roared. "Livy!" Yanking the door open, he found her standing just outside, smiling. "Livy, I've seen a miracle!"

"I know, Youth," she said joyously as she came toward him, "I know."

183

14

ON February 4, 1869, Olivia Lewis Langdon and Samuel Langhorne Clemens became officially engaged. The announcement raised eyebrows among skeptical friends of the Langdons in Elmira, for there was still doubt among the conservative element that a former pilot and miner, presently a wandering platform speaker, would make a proper mate for the daughter of an old and wealthy family, despite the fact that Mark was a "lion" throughout the country. The faith of both of Livy's parents, however, remained steadfast.

Mark gave Livy a plain gold ring instead of one containing a diamond, explaining to her that it was "typical of her future life—namely, that she would have to flourish on substance, rather than luxuries."

Concluding his lecture tour in March, he hastened back to Elmira, where he and his fiancée-editor gave a final polish to the revised proofs of his book. In June *The Innocents Abroad* went to press in an edition of twenty thousand. The first copy was delivered late in

July, and the book was an instant success. By the end of the year, thirty-one thousand copies had been sold at the price of $3.50, a new record for a book of travel.

Despite the universal popularity of *The Innocents,* Mark still did not consider himself an author but a journalist. Looking forward to the comforts of a home and family life, he sought an association with a newspaper and finally had an opportunity to buy a third interest in the *Buffalo Express,* which he acquired with the help of a generous loan from Jervis Langdon.

In his opening piece as a contributing editor Mark assured the newspaper's readers: ". . . I shall never use profanity except when discussing house rent and taxes. . . . I shall not often meddle with politics, because we have a political editor who is already excellent and only needs to serve a term or two in the penitentiary to be perfect. I shall not write any poetry unless I conceive a spite against the subscribers."

Livy and Mark settled upon February 2, 1870, as the date for their wedding. No honeymoon was planned, Mark preferring first to relieve himself of his debts. They decided to go immediately to Buffalo following the ceremony, to take up residence in a small house on Seneca Street.

No wedding day could have begun more auspiciously, for Mark received a $4,000 check, representing three months' royalties on the sales of his book. His happiness was enhanced by the presence of Jane Clemens, and Joe and Harmony Twichell arrived from

185

Hartford, Joe to conduct the wedding ceremony in association with the Rev. Thomas K. Beecher.

The service took place in the Langdons' drawing room, followed by a wedding supper in the dining room for a group of relatives and close friends. While toasts to Livy and Mark were being drunk in pure cold water, Barney cautiously entered the front door carrying an immense floral wreath. It was crowned by two dolls dressed as bride and groom and bore the gold-lettered wish: GOOD LUCK! Leaving his tribute in the center of the flower-decked room, Barney tiptoed out, closing the door noiselessly.

Following a final toast to the bride and a burst of applause, Jane Clemens came from the dining room on the arms of Dan Slote and Jack Van Nostrand.

"Well, Mother Clemens," Dan was saying, "how do you feel about all this? Do you think your little Sammy's in good hands?"

Jane looked up at him. "I know he is. He drank that last toast in water, without makin' a sick face."

Jack shook his head gloomily. "Another good man ruined by a good woman."

Olivia and Jervis Langdon appeared, followed by Charlie, who spied the wreath. "Hey, look at that! Barney's been here."

"My stars," Jane exclaimed. "Just look there, Mrs. Langdon. Have you ever seen anything so handsome?"

"No, Mrs. Clemens, I haven't," Olivia said pleasantly. "It's lovely."

Jervis turned and called: "Livy—Samuel—come out here and see what Barney's brought you."

The bridal couple appeared, hand in hand, followed by a group of guests. "What is it, Father?" Livy asked.

Jervis pointed. "A magnificent floral tribute."

"Oh, dear," Livy said sincerely, "I'm touched." She turned to Mark. "Wasn't that sweet of Barney?"

"Yes," Mark said, "he has a heart of gold—and the soul of an undertaker."

She waggled a finger under his nose. "Now, Youth, you promised to behave."

He caught her finger and held it. "The word was 'obey,' not 'behave.'"

Jack Van Nostrand joined them. "You'll never change this fellow, Livy. He'll always be a sinner."

"Don't listen to Jack," Mark said. "He never did think I had any prospects of salvation."

Livy squeezed his arm. "Well, my husband, if you're to be lost, I want to be lost with you."

Jane spoke to Olivia in her son's defense. "Don't you fret about Sam—he's a lot better than he sounds."

Olivia smiled. "I know that—I'm not the least bit worried."

Dan Slote moved into the circle. "Say, I think it's high time Jack and I legalized this union. Mark, have we your permission to kiss the bride?"

Mark stepped back. "Help yourself, Dan—as long as you don't bestow the same doubtful favor on me."

The two young men kissed Livy's cheeks.

"I'd like to kiss you, Samuel," Olivia said. "May I?"

Mark nodded. "I'd be proud if you did, Mother Langdon."

"Bless you, son," Olivia murmured, brushing his cheek with her lips. "I'm very happy tonight."

"For saying that, I bless you," Mark said.

Jane Clemens stepped up to Livy. "Now, little girl, *I'd* like to kiss you."

"Please do, Mother Clemens."

Jane bussed Livy, then Mark. "You, too, you young scamp."

Mark shook his head. "I swear there hasn't been so much kissing since Romeo shinnied up that drainpipe."

"I've no doubts about your choice now, Sammy," Jane told him. "This sweet child is good enough for you."

"You hear that, Livy?" Mark said. "For the first time in my life I've done something that Ma didn't want to wallop me for."

"If he don't treat you right, daughter," Jane said, "*you* wallop him."

Dan had been conversing with Charlie. "Say, Mark," he said, "Charlie tells me you two are going to live in Buffalo."

"That's right, Dan. I've rented a house there, with gas and inside plumbing."

Dan was delighted. "I'll be in Buffalo next month. Livy, may I drop in for a free dinner?"

"Yes, if you can stand a new bride's cooking."

"I'll take a chance. What's the address?"

"One fifty-eight Seneca Street," Mark told him. "Very fancy part of town."

Livy signaled to her father, who stepped to Mark's side. "I heard what you just said, Samuel. You must be getting absent-minded. It isn't Seneca Street, it's Delaware Avenue."

"I beg your pardon," Mark said, "it's Seneca Street."

"Nonsense," Jervis said gruffly, "you're going to live on Delaware Avenue." He handed Mark a folded document. "If you demand proof, here it is."

Mark opened it, frowning. "This paper looks dangerously legal. Is it a summons?"

Dan looked over Mark's shoulder. "It's a deed to a house."

Livy was bursting to give explanations. "That's right —a house on Delaware Avenue. It's completely furnished—there's even a Maltese cat."

Mark was thoroughly puzzled. "Livy, what in tarnation are you talking about?"

Her eyes were glowing. "Oh, Youth, don't you understand? It's ours—a lovely home—a wedding gift from Father."

Mark frowned. "But—I thought he was giving us tablespoons."

"I did," Jervis said. "You'll find them in the silver drawer when you arrive." He took Mark's hand and pressed it warmly. "Samuel, I wish you eternal happiness in your new home."

"Thank you, sir, thank you," Mark said, truly moved. "With Livy *and* a Maltese cat I'll be in paradise." He slipped his arm around Livy's waist. "Mrs. Clemens, we own real estate. Did you know about our windfall?"

"Of course I did, Youth—we've been planning it for a long time. We've all known about it but you."

"Well, I'll be jiggered," Mark muttered, "and that's the frozen, petrified truth." Clearing his throat, he turned to Jervis. "Father Langdon, I'm so moved by your generosity I can't find words to thank you properly. But I will say this: Whenever you're in Buffalo— no matter if it's twice a year—be sure and look us up. You can even bring your toothbrush and spend the night if you want to—it won't cost you a goldern cent."